George Brown, CLASS CLOWN

Keep On Burpin'

by Nancy Krulik

illustrated by Aaron Blecha

Grosset & Dunlap

An Imprint of Penguin Group (USA) Inc.

GROSSET & DUNLAP
Published by the Penguin Group
Penguin Group (USA) Inc., 375 Hudson Street,
New York, New York 10014, USA
Penguin Group (Canada), 90 Eglinton Avenue East, Suite 700,
Toronto, Ontario M4P 2Y3, Canada
(a division of Pearson Penguin Canada Inc.)
Penguin Books Ltd., 80 Strand, London WC2R 0RL, England
Penguin Group Ireland, 25 St. Stephen's Green, Dublin 2, Ireland
(a division of Penguin Books Ltd.)
Penguin Group (Australia), 250 Camberwell Road,
Camberwell, Victoria 3124, Australia
(a division of Pearson Australia Group Pty. Ltd.)
Penguin Books India Pvt. Ltd., 11 Community Centre,
Panchsheel Park, New Delhi—110 017, India
Penguin Group (NZ), 67 Apollo Drive,
Rosedale, Auckland 0632, New Zealand
(a division of Pearson New Zealand Ltd.)
Penguin Books (South Africa) (Pty.) Ltd., 24 Sturdee Avenue,
Rosebank, Johannesburg 2196, South Africa

Penguin Books Ltd., Registered Offices:
80 Strand, London WC2R 0RL, England

Text copyright © 2011 by Nancy Krulik.
Illustrations copyright © 2011 by Aaron Blecha.
All rights reserved. The books in this bind-up were originally published in 2011 by
Grosset & Dunlap as *What's Black and White and Stinks All Over?*,
Wet and Wild!, and *Help! I'm Stuck in a Giant Nostril!*. This edition published
in 2012 by Grosset & Dunlap, a division of Penguin Young Readers Group,
345 Hudson Street, New York, New York 10014.
GROSSET & DUNLAP is a trademark of Penguin Group (USA) Inc.
Printed in the U.S.A.

The Library of Congress has catalogued the individual books under the following Control
Numbers: 2010029432 (#4 *What's Black and White and Stinks All Over?*), 2010040830
(#5 *Wet and Wild!*), 2011000845 (#6 *Help! I'm Stuck in a Giant Nostril!*)

ISBN 978-0-448-46285-1   10 9 8 7 6 5 4 3 2 1

For Amanda and Ian, with thanks for all the light and laughter.—NK

For Betsy Boo—my Burpin' inspiration and more—AB

George Brown, CLASS CLOWN

What's **Black** and **White** and **Stinks** All Over?

by Nancy Krulik
illustrated by Aaron Blecha

Grosset & Dunlap
An Imprint of Penguin Group (USA) Inc.

Chapter 1

Eeerrroooooo!

George Brown covered his ears as feedback from the school intercom exploded into his classroom.

"I think **my ears are bleeding**," George told his friend Alex.

"I'm surprised the noise didn't crack a window," Alex agreed.

"Good morning, students of Edith B. Sugarman Elementary School." The voice of the principal, Mrs. McKeon, was coming through on the intercom. "Here

are your morning announcements: Today's lunch is Salisbury steak."

"Oh man," Alex said. **"Not mystery meat again."**

Salisbury steak was gross. It was always gray and dry. And no matter how much **brown, gooey sauce** was poured over it, it always tasted like cardboard covered in slimy mud.

"First-grade library books should be returned by Friday," the principal continued. "And all third-graders need to remember that their bake sale is next week."

George **started picking dirt** out from under his fingernails. Morning announcements were *so* boring.

"And don't forget, the fourth-grade Field Day is tomorrow," Mrs. McKeon added. "Everyone should arrive at Beaver

Brook Park at nine o'clock sharp. Wear your team shirts and come ready for fun."

George stopped picking at his nails and grinned. This was going to be his first Field Day at his new school. He figured it would be pretty cool.

"What are you smiling about?" Louie, the tall kid who sat near George, whispered. **"Field Day stinks."**

"Come on," George whispered back. "We're going to be outside all day. And we don't get any homework tonight."

"Trust me," Louie said. "It's just a bunch of dumb races and a lousy boxed lunch."

"Yeah, dumb races," Louie's friend Mike said.

"Lousy lunch," Louie's other friend Max added.

George looked over at Alex.

"Louie's right," Alex told George. "And

it usually rains on Field Day, too."

"Please keep it down," their teacher, Mrs. Kelly, said. "Mrs. McKeon hasn't finished all the announcements."

"And now for some big news," Mrs. McKeon continued. "This Friday will be the last time you hear me on the school intercom."

George started to clap and dance around—until he remembered he didn't want to be the class clown anymore. **Those days were over.**

"Starting on Monday, you will find television sets in all of your classrooms," the principal said. "Our school is going to have its own closed-circuit TV station. There will be a studio set up in the audiovisual room. We will be able to broadcast from that studio directly to every classroom in the school!"

George's eyes popped open. A school

TV station. Okay, so maybe this was **a *little* exciting**.

"The reporters on our new school station will be you—the students," Mrs. McKeon said. "We need writers, camera people, and broadcasters. Anyone interested in being part of WEBS TV should stop by the school office at recess today and sign up."

"Webs TV?" George asked. "What kind of name is that?"

"Not webs," Louie said with a laugh. "W-E-B-S. As in W-Edith B. Sugarman TV. Don't you know anything?"

George did know something. He knew Louie was a **class-A jerk**. But he didn't

say that out loud. Teachers got mad when you said stuff like that. And George was trying really hard not to have any teachers at his new school get mad at him.

George was an expert at being the new kid in school because his dad was in the army, and his family moved around a lot. Up until now, he'd been the class clown at every single school.

This time, though, George was turning over a new leaf. **No more pranks.** No more trips to the principal's office. **No more trouble.**

At first, it really worked. George raised his hand before answering questions. He didn't make faces or laugh behind teachers' backs. He didn't even squirt Jell-O between his teeth and pretend it was blood.

George wasn't causing any trouble. And the **trouble with that** was that the kids all thought he was the boring new guy. But that wasn't the real George **at all**.

Then after his first day at his new school, George's parents took him out to Ernie's Ice Cream Emporium. While they were sitting outside and George was drinking his root beer float, a shooting star flashed across the sky. So George made a wish:

I want to make kids laugh—but not get into trouble.

Unfortunately, the star was gone before George could finish the wish. So only half came true—the first half.

As soon as George had finished his float, **he got a funny feeling in his belly**. It was like hundreds of tiny bubbles were bouncing around in there. The bubbles bounced up and down and all around. They **ping-ponged** their way into his chest and **bing-bonged** their way up into his throat. And then . . .

George let out a big burp. **A *huge* super burp.**

The super burp was loud, and it was *magic*.

Suddenly George lost control of his

arms and legs. It was like they had minds of their own. His hands grabbed straws and stuck them up his nose like a walrus. His feet jumped up on the table and started dancing the **hokey pokey**. Everyone at Ernie's started laughing—except George's parents, who were covered in the ice cream he had knocked over.

That wasn't the only time the super burp had burst its way out of George's belly. There had been plenty of **magic gas attacks** since then. Once, the burp made him dive-bomb off the stage during the school talent show—which would have been cool if he hadn't landed right in Principal McKeon's lap.

The burp was always popping up when George least expected it. Like the time it came in the middle of his science project and forced him to make his **model volcano** explode all over the classroom. Or the time during the backyard circus when the burp made George jump on a trampoline. He kept bouncing up and down until suddenly, somehow, his underwear got caught on a tree branch. George just hung there with the **world's worst wedgie**. His rear end still hurt whenever he thought about it!

To make matters worse, Louie always made fun of George for the things the burp made him do. Goofing on George was Louie's favorite hobby. George didn't know why Louie hated him so much. **But Louie did hate him.** He'd even thrown George out of his band—for no reason at all, except that he hated George.

Which was actually kind of okay, because George wasn't too crazy about Louie, either. In fact, Louie was the **worst thing** about living in Beaver Brook. Well, except for the magic super burp.

Chapter 2

"What are you guys signing up for?" George asked Alex and Chris as they headed toward the school office after lunch.

"Cameraman," Alex said.

"I want to be a news reporter," Chris said.

George looked down and scraped some **Salisbury steak goo from his shirt**. Then he popped his finger in his mouth. *Yuck.*

It still tasted like brown, gooey slime. But what tasted even worse than the goo? **The goo mixed with shirt lint.**

George gagged a little and swallowed. Then he said, "I think I'd make a good sportscaster."

"Why?" Chris asked.

"I love skateboarding," George said. "That counts as a sport."

"Yeah, but you'd have to report on the school basketball team and the track team," Alex told him. "We don't have a skateboard team."

"I was on the track team at my old school," George said. He didn't add that he usually came in last in every race. **That was the one good thing about being the new kid.** No one in your new school had to know any of the embarrassing junk that happened at your old school.

In the school office, a **really tall** sixth-grader came over to George and his friends. "Are you guys here to sign up for the TV station?" he asked.

Alex said, "I was thinking about being a cameraman."

"We still have a couple of spots open," the kid said. "And since you're a fourth-grader, you can work the cameras. No one in the lower grades is allowed to."

"Cool," Alex said. "What do I do?"

The kid pointed to sign-up sheets that were taped to the wall. "Write your name on the one that says CAMERAS."

"Do you still need news reporters?" Chris asked.

"Do you have any experience?" the big sixth-grader asked.

Chris didn't say anything. George could tell he was kind of scared. The sixth-grader was huge.

"Chris is a *great* writer," George piped up. "He writes comic books. They're about this **superhero** named **Toiletman**, who uses a plunger to flush out trouble."

The sixth-grader frowned. "Writing news stories is different from writing comic stories about a guy with a plunger."

"A *superhero* with a plunger," George corrected him.

"Whatever." The kid looked at Chris. "I guess we could give you a try," he said finally.

As Chris wrote his name on the sign-up sheet, George swallowed hard and said, "I'd really like to be a sportscaster."

"You and about a billion other kids," the sixth-grader said. "There's only going

to be one sportscaster from each grade."

"Has anybody else from the fourth grade signed up?" George asked. Then, out of the corner of his eye, George spotted Louie coming into the school office. He was with Mike and Max, just like always.

"Okay, I already signed my name on the sheet," Louie told the sixth-grader. "So when can I do my first sportscast?"

Oh man. Louie had beaten him to the sign-up sheet.

"Not so fast," the sixth-grader said. "This kid here wants the job; other kids do, too."

Louie glared at George. **"He doesn't have the experience I have,"** he told the sixth-grader.

"What experience?" George asked him.

"My brother, Sam, is the sportscaster at the middle school TV station," Louie explained.

"It's a family thing," Mike said.

"Kind of like big noses," Max said. "Not that you have a big nose or anything, Louie," he added quickly.

"We've gotta make this fair," the sixth-grader said.

"Well, I got here first," Louie said. "So I'm the sportscaster, **fair and square**."

"You eat faster than me is all," George said. "So you got here quicker."

Just then Principal McKeon walked out of her office. "What's the problem, boys?"

"They both want to be the fourth-grade sportscaster," the big kid explained.

Mrs. McKeon nodded. "Well, how about making an **audition tape**?"

"How would we do that?" George asked her.

"Tomorrow is Field Day," Mrs. McKeon said. "Anyone who wants to be the fourth-grade sportscaster should report on the events."

"How are we supposed to report on the races when we're running in them?" George asked.

Mrs. McKeon said, "You can report on the races you aren't taking part in. You can interview your friends, too."

"That sounds fair," George said.

The sixth-grader shrugged. "Okay. After I watch the tapes, I'll decide who made **the best one**, and that kid gets the job."

George held his hand out to Louie. "May the best man win."

"Oh, I will," Louie said.

"Yeah, he will," Max added.

"Definitely," Mike agreed. "Louie always wins."

George smiled. *Not this time,* he thought.

Chapter 3

When George arrived at Beaver Brook Park the next morning, he saw Louie showing Mike how to use a fancy video camera. It was the kind of video camera that could shoot things from far away and close-up. It seemed like Mike was having a really tough time learning how to use it.

It wasn't right that **such a jerk** had so much cool stuff. Louie had been the first kid in the grade to get **sneakers with wheels on them**. He was the first one to get a scooter with a motor on it. And now he was the first kid to have a superdeluxe video camera.

"You better take real good care of that camera," Louie told Mike. "It's my brother, Sam's."

"I will," Mike promised. "I swear."

"And make sure you point the camera at me **a lot**, and use that close-up lens," Louie told him. "This is *my* audition tape."

"Close-ups, got it," Mike said.

"What can I do, Louie?" Max asked.

Louie thought for a minute. "You make sure my hair looks good and stuff like that while Mike is shooting me."

Max nodded. "You can count on me!"

he said. "You can have my napkin at lunch, too, so you don't get any stains on your shirt."

"All my folks had was this old camera," Alex said to George. "My mom got it when I was born."

"It's okay," George said. "You're definitely going to be a better cameraman than Mike. Besides, it's not how good the camera is. It's how good the *sportscaster* is. Who are people going to want to get their sports news from—a cool kid like me or a **pain in the neck** like Louie?"

Just then Sage snuck up behind George and Alex. "**Georgie**, I heard you're trying to be a sportscaster," she said. "I'm in the wheelbarrow race. Do you want to interview me now?"

George turned around. Sage was tilting her head and giving him a goofy smile.

"Well, uh . . . **no thanks**," George mumbled. "Maybe later."

"I'm so glad we're on the same team," Sage continued, pointing to her T-shirt. It was green with white letters that said VIPERS, just like George's shirt. "I don't like snakes. But I'll wear the shirt proudly **because *you're* wearing it, too**."

At first, George thought he was lucky to be on the Vipers, especially since Alex

and Chris had wound up on that team, too. But now that George knew Sage was on his team, **he wasn't so cool with it anymore**.

Then again, at least he wasn't on the other team, **the Sharks**, with Louie, Max, and Mike. George's friend Julianna was on their team, though.

Too bad the Vipers couldn't trade Sage for Julianna. She was a lot cooler

than Sage was. She was also **a lot faster** than just about anyone in the fourth grade. A kid like Julianna could win Field Day for her team.

"Boys and girls, gather around!" Principal McKeon shouted through her megaphone. "It's time to start the Field Day festivities."

"What's Principal McKeon doing here?" George asked Chris and Alex.

"Since your gym teacher, Mr. Trainer, is absent today—," Mrs. McKeon continued.

George started to laugh. The whole time George had been at Edith B. Sugarman Elementary School, he'd only seen Mr. Trainer a couple of times. The guy was always absent.

"I am going to lead you kids in a **special sun salutation**," Mrs. McKeon said.

Sage started hopping up and down like she had just heard the best news in the world. "Oh yay!" she cheered. "I love yoga. **You get to twist your body into all sorts of shapes.** The sun salutation is tough, though."

Just then, Louie came running over. Mike and Max were right behind him.

"So, you know how to do this yoga pose, Sage?" Louie asked.

Louie was making his voice sound really low. George figured he was trying to sound like a real sportscaster.

"I take classes," Sage told him. "And I'm really good. Yoga helps you to be at one with nature, **which is perfect**, since we're out here with all this nature around."

George wanted to stick his finger down his throat and pretend he was puking, but he didn't. If the principal saw him, she'd be mad. **And he was trying really hard not to get in trouble.**

Sage showed the kids a couple of yoga poses. "This is cobra," she said as she got down on her belly and lifted her head like a snake.

"Film her!" Louie snapped at Mike.

Rats. George had to admit Louie had beaten him to **the first scoop of the day**.

Not that he was sure yoga counted as a sport. *But still.*

"Okay, kids," Mrs. Kelly said as she walked over to where Sage was demonstrating her **downward-facing dog**. "Let's all gather around Mrs. McKeon so we can do our sun salutations."

George looked at Mrs. Kelly's T-shirt.
It had green and white stripes on it. Mrs.
McKeon was wearing the same shirt, and
so was Mrs. Miller, the other fourth-grade
teacher. George figured that showed that
the teachers and the principal **weren't
taking sides**.

"Okay, fourth-graders, first we stand
up straight with our hands together," Mrs.
McKeon explained as she started the sun
salutation. "Next
we reach up high
toward the sun . . ."

George tried
to follow the yoga
poses his principal
was doing.

**The hardest one
was downward-
facing dog.**

George tried to bend over and stick his rear end in the air like a dog stretching after a nap. But he couldn't. He was too freaked out by **the bubbles starting to fizz in his belly**.

George could tell there was a burp brewing down there. And not just any burp. From the way those bubbles were bing-bonging their way around his belly, George could tell this was a *super burp*. And that was *ba-a-ad*!

George was going to have to fight with all his might to keep it down. Because if **George couldn't squelch this belch**, there was going to be trouble!

The last thing George wanted was for the super burp to escape in front of the whole fourth grade. He clamped his lips tight and sucked in his belly as hard as he could. And then . . .

BUUURP!

George let out the loudest burp anyone had ever heard. It was so loud **you could hear it on the sun**!

The kids all turned around to stare at him. George opened his mouth and tried to say "excuse me." But all that came out was, *"Ruff! Ruff!"*

It wasn't George's fault. It was his *mouth's* fault. But it didn't want to apologize. It wanted to bark like a

downward-facing dog.

"*Ruff! Ruff!*"

George ordered himself to stand up and act **normally**. But that didn't happen. Instead, George stayed down on all fours. He ran over to a tree. Then he lifted his leg and pretended to be **a dog peeing on the tree**.

The kids' mouths all hung open. *Was this really happening?*

"George Brown!" Principal McKeon shouted. "That's not funny!"

"*Arooo!*" George howled.

He rolled over in the grass.

He sat up on his hind legs. He pushed his tongue out of his mouth, held his arms out like a dog, and begged.

The kids all laughed harder.

"Stop that right now!" Principal McKeon shouted.

"*Yip! Yip!*" George barked.

His arms and legs raced over to Principal McKeon. **And then George's tongue did the worst thing EVER.**

It licked Principal McKeon's hand! **Gross!** Now George had principal germs in his mouth. But George's tongue didn't care. It just kept licking.

And then . . . suddenly . . . *Whoosh!* George felt a huge bubble **pop** inside his stomach. All the air rushed right out of him.

The super burp was gone.

But George was still there. He let out a little whimper—kind of like a puppy saying he was sorry. But it was too late to apologize.

From the look on Principal McKeon's face, George could tell **he was in trouble**. *Big* trouble. He wasn't sure what punishment the principal was going to dish out. But he was pretty sure it would be *ruff*.

Chapter 4

George was sitting on a rock with his head in his hands. "She's **calling my parents tonight**," George told Alex. "They'll probably **ground me for a week**." George groaned. "And she penalized our team two points."

"That was severe," Alex said. "All you did was bark a little."

George knew that wasn't all he'd done. Alex was just trying to make him feel better.

But **the worst part** was that Louie was interviewing kids about George. "So, what just happened out there?" Louie asked Julianna.

"I think George was trying to psych out our team," Julianna said. "He wanted us to think he was a **wild, crazy dog** who was

dangerous. But we're the Sharks. We're not afraid of anyone."

Louie smiled. Then he turned to Chris and Alex. **"Hey, did you know our team has a secret weapon?** It's George. As long as he's on your side, *we're* sure to win."

That really cracked up Mike and Max. Mike laughed so hard, he almost dropped the video camera.

Louie shot him an angry look. Mike stopped laughing. Fast.

George pretended to ignore Louie. He turned to watch some other kids get ready at the starting line for the **wheelbarrow race**. Chris was the wheelbarrow, and Sage was holding his legs.

Mrs. McKeon blew her whistle and the kids took off down the field. It was an exciting race. It could actually make a good story for his sportscast audition tape.

"Alex, turn on the camera and follow me," he said.

Alex grabbed the camera and began filming George as he ran along the side of the field.

"There's Sage pushing Chris as hard as she can," George said, **sounding like a real sportscaster**. "Notice how straight Chris is holding his legs. That's how the professional wheelbarrow racers do it."

George asked Alex to switch his camera angle. "Oh, look! Louie and

Julianna are coming up from the rear. Julianna is the wheelbarrow and she's working hard at walking on her hands. But Louie has just dropped her legs. *Oooh.* Belly flop! **That had to hurt**."

George and Alex ran ahead to watch the winners crossing the finish line. "Watch out, Sage and Chris," he said into the camera. "Louie and Julianna are right beside you. **It's anyone's race now!**"

A split second later, Sage, Chris, Louie, and Julianna all made it to the finish line.

"We won!" Sage and Chris shouted excitedly.

"We won!" Louie and Julianna shouted excitedly.

"I think it was a tie," Mrs. McKeon told the kids.

George said, "Look, **Alex shot the whole thing**. We were filming the race. That will show who won."

"Terrific, George," Mrs. Kelly told him. "Principal McKeon and I will watch the tape now."

Alex handed over his camera, and a few moments later, Mrs. McKeon said, **"Well, this decides it.** Sage's hand crossed the finish line just a second before Julianna's. Chris and Sage are the winners. Good reporting, George."

As soon as Mrs. Kelly and Principal McKeon had walked away, Louie gave George an angry look.

"I bet you **got yourself kicked out** of the race on purpose."

"Why would I do that?" George asked.

"Because you want to be the sportscaster," Louie said. "**That was probably the most exciting race of the day.** I was racing so I couldn't report on it."

George grinned. That was true. And there was nothing Louie could do about it.

Chapter 5

"Go-o-o-o-o Vipers!" George and Chris
gave each other a high five as **George
crossed the finish line**—just seconds
ahead of Louie—in the final leg of the relay
race. Now George had made up those two
points he'd lost for the Vipers earlier.

And the best part was that Alex had picked up the camera **just in time** to film George winning for his team. George would be able to use his own victory in his audition tape. **Sweet!**

Soon it was time for the next race. A large, brown suitcase was placed on the ground in front of each team. "What's that for?" George asked his teammates.

"A race," Sage told him.

George rolled his eyes. *No duh.* "What *kind* of race?"

"I don't have a clue," Alex said.

Just then, Mrs. McKeon picked up a megaphone. She looked at the Vipers. Then she looked at the Sharks. "Okay, fourth-graders," she said. "For this race, one person on each team has to be *it*. Are there any volunteers?"

George smiled. Here was his chance to really get everyone on his good side.

He would volunteer to be *it*—even though **he had no real idea** what he was volunteering for.

"Me. I'll do it," he told the other Vipers.

"I'll be *it* for the Sharks," Julianna volunteered. She smiled over at George. "It's you against me."

"The object of this race is to dress the person who is *it*," Mrs. McKeon continued. "You must put **every piece of clothing in the suitcase** on him or her. And then, once that person is dressed, he or she has to run to the finish line."

George smiled. That didn't sound too hard.

But the minute Mrs. Kelly blew her whistle and Alex opened the suitcase, **George knew he was in trouble**. There weren't just any clothes inside the suitcase. There were *lady's* clothes:

a dress, a pocketbook, a shawl, a curly
blond wig, and **worst of all** . . . high
heels. Was George actually supposed to
run in them?

The minute the whistle blew, Chris
picked up a yellow and red flowered dress
and shoved it over George's head. **"Suck
in your gut, George,"** Chris told him. **"I
gotta zip this thing."**

"Okay, here's your shawl," Sage
said. "Oh, I love how you look in purple,
George."

Alex dumped the wig on George's
head. "Wow! You're a blonde!"

"**Ha-ha. Very funny,**" George said as he slipped on the high-heeled shoes.

"**Now grab your pocketbook and run!**" Chris said. He started to laugh. "Man, that sounds hilarious."

George could barely walk. And he couldn't see. He took two steps. *Whoops!* He fell backward **right onto his rear end**. But he scrambled up, straightened his wig, held tight to his purse, and kept on hobbling toward the finish line.

Once or twice he looked back. Thank goodness Julianna wasn't having any better luck than George. She was falling all over the place, too.

"Come on, George, just a few more feet!" Alex shouted.

George **huffed** and **puffed**. He pushed the wig out of his eyes. He put **one heel in front of the other**.

Ooomph. George fell right on his belly.

He reached his arms out to break his fall. And then . . .

"We have a winner!" Mrs. McKeon shouted. "George's hand has just crossed the finish line. The Vipers win!"

George looked up. Through the

strands of yellow wig-hair he could see his teammates **cheering wildly**.

He could also see Louie. He was yelling at Mike and pointing at George. "Not me!" Louie shouted. "Point the camera at George!"

As Mike videotaped George, Louie began talking in his sportscaster voice. "It was close. Julianna would have won, if George—or should I call him *Georgina*—hadn't **belly flopped** over the finish line."

As Mike turned off the camera, Louie

shoved his face right into George's and shot him a mean grin. "This is going to be the best **sports blooper tape** anyone has ever made! I can't wait until the whole school sees it."

Blooper tape! So that was what Louie was up to. He was using this sportscaster contest as another excuse to make fun of George.

Grrr . . .

Chapter 6

"There goes Chris!" George announced as Alex filmed the **egg-on-a-spoon** race. "He's gaining on Mike. Oops. Chris lost his egg. And this race goes to the Sharks."

Chris was not smiling after he crossed the finish line a couple of feet behind Mike. "That's harder than it looks," he told George and Alex.

"Don't worry, dude," George told him. "The next race is the three-legged race. I did that with my dad at an army base picnic. **I can win it for us.**"

Just then, Sage walked over to George. She had a thick rope in her hands. "I'll be your partner, George," she said. Then she **batted her eyelashes** up and down. It made her look like she had spider legs hanging from her eyelids. *Yuck!*

Mrs. Kelly flashed one of her **big, gummy smiles** at George and Sage. "How nice!" she said. "I didn't know you two were such good friends."

George was really stuck now. He was going to have to touch Sage—*ugh!*—whether he liked it or not.

A few minutes later, George and Sage hobbled **arm in arm** over to the starting line, right next to Louie and Max. Louie looked over and flashed George a big smile. George didn't know why.

"Okay, everyone," Principal McKeon said. **"On your mark . . . get set . . . go!"**

George and Sage took off down the field. They were going pretty fast, too. At least they were until George felt something fizzy in his belly.

Oh no! Not the **super burp**!

But it *was* the super burp. It was back, and **it wanted out**. Already it was

ping-ponging its way out of George's belly, and **bing-bonging** its way into his chest.

This could get really *ba-a-ad!*

George had to keep the burp down. It had already gotten him in trouble once today. **Once was enough.**

George shut his mouth tight. He started banging on his chest. Maybe he could **break up the burp** and push it back down into his belly.

Oomph! George hit himself again and lost his balance.

To keep from falling, George grabbed on to **whatever was closest**—which happened to be Sage.

Sage wrapped her arms around George and gave him a squeeze. **"Oh, Georgie!"**

Everyone was looking!

This was terrible. Horrible. Awful.

Whoosh! Suddenly George felt a huge bubble pop inside his stomach. All the air rushed right out of him. **The fizzy feeling was gone.**

Louie and Mike won the race. But at least George had squelched the belch!

Sage was smiling. She batted her eyelashes up and down. "I knew you liked me," she told him, and gave him a hug.

George groaned. The belch was gone, but Sage was **making him sick** to his stomach.

"Did you get all of it on camera?" Louie was asking Mike. "Me winning *and* that clown freaking out again?" Louie was pointing at George.

"Every second," Mike said proudly. "Even the hug."

"I wasn't hugging her!" George insisted as he untied himself from Sage.

"You were, too!" Sage said. **Then she stormed off.**

George tried to look on the bright side. The **really important thing** was that he'd managed to beat the burp. And as an added bonus, maybe now Sage would leave him alone.

Score one for George!

Chapter 7

"Dude, what came over you? You were **definitely acting weird** out there," Alex told George as the boys took their boxed lunches to a far corner of the field.

"You'd act weird, too, if you were tied to Sage," George said as he plopped on the ground. He opened the cardboard box and looked inside. *Yuck!*

He picked up the squished pieces of bread. "What's inside this?"

Chris took a look at his sandwich. "At first I thought it was egg salad because **there's something yellow in it**," he said. "But now I'm not so sure."

"What are those gray spots on the bread?" Alex asked.

"Better not to know," George answered.

"I think that piece of celery just moved," Chris said.

George looked down at Chris's sandwich. **"Dude, I don't think that's celery,"** he said, and put his sandwich back in the box. "Can I borrow the camera?" he asked Alex.

"Are you going to film people eating?" Chris asked him.

"Eating's not a sport," Alex told Chris.

"It is when you eat this stuff," George joked. "You take a bite and then see how fast you can run to the bathroom to **throw up**."

Alex and Chris laughed.

"Actually, I'm going to interview people about how they think the day is going," George told his friends. "Because so far I only have the wheelbarrow race. And Louie has . . ." George couldn't even finish the sentence. It was that **embarrassing**.

Instead, he pointed the camera at Chris. "So, Chris, can you tell me what the **highlight of the morning** was for you?"

"Well, I kind of liked zipping you into that dress for the race," Chris said with a laugh. "That was hilarious."

George turned the camera away from Chris. Fast. "How about you, Alex?" he asked, pointing the camera at his other best friend.

"It was pretty funny the way you did the downward-facing dog," Alex said. "Licking Principal McKeon's hand—**that took guts**."

This interview was *not* going the way George had hoped.

"Check it out," Chris said. "Louie saw you interviewing us, so now he's interviewing people on his team. **That guy doesn't have an original idea in his head**."

"It doesn't matter," Alex told him. Then

he smiled. "Guess what? Mike forgot to turn the camera on. The little red light isn't flashing now. The **tape's gonna be blank**."

"Louie's going to freak when he realizes Mike's not getting any of this," Chris said.

"I hope so," George said. "Because *that's* something I'd really like to get on tape!"

Chapter 8

"Wow! **This is a race worthy of Toiletman!**" Chris shouted excitedly as he and the other Vipers gathered at the starting line for the first race after lunch.

On the ground in front of each team was **a plunger and three rolls of toilet paper**.

Mrs. McKeon picked up her megaphone.

"This race is always a favorite at Field Day," Mrs. McKeon announced, a big smile on her face. "There will be three contestants from each team. **The first person scoops up a roll of toilet paper onto the plunger end.** Then he or she runs across the field, dumps the toilet paper in the trash bucket, and races back to the starting line so the second person can do the same thing. The first team to get all three rolls into their trash bucket wins!"

"Oh, we're gonna win this one," Chris said. **"Toilet paper is my thing!"**

"Then you should go first," Alex told Chris. "And then maybe Sage can go." Alex turned to a skinny kid with really long legs. "Charlie, you go last. You'll be running against Julianna, which will be hard."

"I think I can beat her," Charlie said.

George smiled. The Vipers just might be able to take this race.

The whistle blew and the race began!

"Chris is off to a great start," George said. "Look at his technique. The roll of toilet paper is sitting right in the middle of the plunger. **He's got it perfectly balanced! What skill!**"

At first, George was smiling for the camera. But then, all of a sudden, he didn't feel like smiling anymore. That fizzy feeling was back. It wasn't just

bing-bonging and ping-ponging its way up to George's mouth. This time it was BING-BONGING and PING-PONGING!

This was a classic battle between man and burp! And it was a fight George was determined to win. Quickly, he grabbed a roll of toilet paper and shoved a wad in his mouth like a cork.

"George, **quit kidding around**," Charlie said. "That toilet paper is for the race."

But George *wasn't* kidding around. **This was serious business.** He stuffed

more and more toilet paper into his mouth. **His cheeks felt like they were about to explode.**

Alex couldn't help himself. He began to laugh really hard.

"Alex, stop laughing!" Sage said. "Chris is almost back with the plunger. I'm next."

George could feel his eyes bulging now. The **burp was really angry**. It was pounding around in George's chest and bouncing up into his throat. *Boing! Boing! Boing!*

The **magic burp** slipped out. It wasn't a huge burp. In fact, as far as super burps went, it was kind of small. But it was powerful enough to shoot the wad of wet, slimy toilet paper **out of George's mouth** and into the air.

Splat! The wad of paper and spit landed **right on the back of Louie's neck**.

"Hey! Who did that?" Louie turned around and glared.

George opened his mouth to say "sorry." But that's not what came out. Instead, George's mouth started to tell jokes.

"Speaking of toilet paper," George's mouth said, "do you guys know why Eeyore looked into the toilet? He wanted to see Pooh!"

Some kids on the Vipers laughed. But most were cheering Sage on. She was running down the field with the **toilet paper sitting on her plunger**. As soon as she reached the starting line, she handed

the plunger off to Charlie. Charlie scooped up the toilet paper on the plunger.

"You guys know what one toilet said to the other?" George asked his teammates. "**You sure you're not sick?** You're looking a little flushed!"

Charlie was running down the field, but he was laughing so hard he dropped the toilet paper . . . twice.

"George, I know you're having fun," Mrs. Kelly said. "But **this is still school**. That kind of joke just isn't appropriate."

"Then **how about this one**?" George's mouth asked. "What game is played in the bathroom?"

"What?" Alex asked.

"Ring Around the Bathtub," George said.

The kids laughed again. Mrs. Kelly said, "I think it's time to stop joking now."

Suddenly, the Sharks began to cheer. Julianna had crossed the finish line. She'd won the race for her team.

Whoosh! Something went pop in the bottom of George's belly. It was like all the air rushed right out of him. The burp was gone.

George opened his mouth to say "sorry." **And that's exactly what came out.** He was sorry that the Vipers had lost the race.

"I hope you're apologizing for spitting toilet paper at me," Louie shouted to George.

George shook his head. "Don't blame me," he said. After all, George hadn't spit anything at anyone. The super burp had **blasted the paper** right out of him.

Louie glared at George. "You're just lucky Mike was running in the race so he couldn't film you. Otherwise, I would prove it was you who spit toilet paper at me."

"I'm not sure who did what," Mrs. Kelly told the boys. "But I'm keeping my eye on you, George Brown. Trouble seems to follow you wherever you go."

George frowned. It wasn't trouble that was following him. **It was gas.**

Chapter 9

"Does everyone have their paint chips?" Alex asked. "The scavenger hunt is worth three points. If we take this, we're the **Field Day champions**."

"All right!" George pumped his fist in the air. His team still had a chance.

George held his white and yellow chips. Each kid had two paint chips in different colors. The idea was to find **something in nature** that matched the colors you were holding.

"Okay, fourth-graders, start hunting!" Mrs. McKeon shouted cheerfully.

Sage showed her orange and purple chips to George. "Purple is going to be hard." She smiled, and started doing that **spider-leg-eyelash-blinking thing again**. "Maybe you can help me."

Yeah, like that was going to happen. George wasn't planning on staying anywhere near Sage. He started running and didn't look back.

When he figured he was far enough away, George stopped and took out his paint chips. Yellow. That shouldn't be too hard. He looked around in the grass until he spotted **a bright yellow dandelion**. It was the exact shade of yellow that he needed. **Oh yeah!** *Score!*

"Yellow dandelion!" George said as he went over to Chris and dropped the weed into the Vipers' brown paper bag his friend was holding.

"And here's a green leaf," Charlie said. He held it next to his paint chip. **"It's an exact match."**

"I've got brown . . . here's some brown . . . *something*," Chris said.

He stared at
what looked like a pile of
dark brown pebbles.
Alex glanced over Chris's shoulder.
"That's poop," he said. He bent down
and took a closer look. **"It probably
comes from a medium-sized
rodent."**

George looked at his
friend in amazement. Alex
was smart. But this was
creepy **smart**. "You can
actually tell what made
this poop?"

"Not exactly," Chris said.
"But judging from the poop's
color and its smell, it's definitely
a rodent. Probably one that eats

bugs, parts of dead birds, and **maybe some garbage**."

"Okay, I think I'm going to throw up," said Sage, who had suddenly appeared.

"Just scoop the poop and stick it in the bag, Chris," George said. "We have to move fast if we're going to win the scavenger hunt."

"I'm not scooping up any poop," Chris said. "You do it."

"No way," George said.

"Don't look at me," Sage told the boys.

"Alex?" George asked. **"You're the poop expert around here."**

"I only look," Alex said. "I don't touch."

"Maybe I'd better find something else **dark brown**," Chris said.

"Look! **There's fungus** on the roots of that tree," George told him. "It's dark brown."

Chris started pointing to the bushes nearby. "Hey, did you guys hear that?" he asked.

"Hear what?" George asked.

The kids all got very quiet. Suddenly **there was some rustling in the bushes**. There was definitely something hiding.

"Maybe it's whatever made that poop," George said.

"Let's go." Sage tugged at George's sleeve. George pulled away from her.

"You think it's **a bear** or something?" Chris asked nervously. "I saw this movie once where a bear tore apart a whole family." Chris started walking in the opposite direction. **"I'm outta here."**

"Good idea," Alex said.

"I'm right behind you," George agreed.

"And I'm right behind *you*, George," Sage said.

George groaned.

Chapter 10

"Mud! Nice, brown mud," Chris shouted. He reached down and scooped up a handful of **slippery, slimy lake mud**, and plopped it into the scavenger hunt bag. "One color closer to victory!"

George hunted all around the edge of the lake for something that was white. Sage found a purple flower, so she was done. Alex found a gray rock and a blue feather. And Charlie had already picked

a red berry from a bush. But nothing white was in sight . . . **it was weird**. Back home in his dresser there were a million things that were white, or sort of white: his socks, his T-shirts, even his **tighty-whitey underpants**. Out here, nothing.

George sat down on a hollow log to think. But before he could investigate further, he heard a loud, rumbling sound. And that was scary because of where it was coming from.

The rumbling was coming from George's belly—along with a terrible, fizzy feeling. The kind of feeling George always got when he **let loose a mighty, mega, magical super burp**.

Oh no! He was setting **some sort of record** for magic burps in a single day! Already it was ping-ponging its way out of George's belly and bing-bonging its way into his chest.

George wasn't about to surrender to the burp. He **clamped his mouth shut** and **sucked in his stomach** as hard as he could. He spun around and around in a circle, trying to force the burp into his feet like water down a drain.

The spinning was a bad move. Now,
besides feeling fizzy, George felt dizzy.

Sage went running over. "George, are
you okay?" she asked.

George stared right at Sage and . . .

B·U·U·U·R·P!

He let out a **massive** burp.

"Gross!" Sage shouted.

George opened his mouth to
say "excuse me." But that's
not what came out. Instead,

George shouted, "CANNONBALL!"

George's legs sprang into action. They raced to the lake. And then, **with one powerful leap**, his legs catapulted him into it.

"Yo, dude, get out of there," Alex called. "We've got a job to do!"

George wanted to get out of the water. He really did. **But George wasn't in charge of George now.** The super burp was. And it had other plans.

George's body ducked down under the water. A moment later, he popped back up and began **spitting a stream of water** right out of his mouth. He was a giant George fountain. Now kids from the other team came to watch the *George Show*.

As soon as **the George fountain was empty,** George's legs ran out of the lake and onto the shore. Chris was shouting and pointing at something . . .

George shook the water out of his ears. Now he could hear. Chris was shouting, **"Skunk!"**

Kids scattered as fast as their legs would take them. All except for George.

Skunks were black . . . and white! Maybe he could get **some white skunk hair** and win the scavenger hunt for his team.

Part of George's brain knew this was crazy thinking. But the burp had taken over his mind now, too! He scurried over to the skunk.

The skunk glared at George. George glared back. All he needed was one skunk hair. He reached out . . . and the skunk turned around and **pointed its black-and-white-striped tush** right at George. Then it raised its tail and **let out a spray.**

Whoosh! George felt something go pop in his belly—**like a pin going into a balloon**. All the air seemed to just rush right out of him.

The super burp was gone . . . but the smell of the **skunk spray** was not!

George stank, stunk, or however you say it . . . "Oh man," he groaned. **He was wet, smelly, and miserable.**

Just when George thought nothing could be worse, he heard a noise coming from nearby.

And then something awful emerged from behind the bushes. Something worse than a bear. **Worse than a wild coyote. Even worse than a skunk.**

It was a *Louie*!

"George, that was awesome!" Louie shouted. "Mike, did you get that?" he asked.

Mike popped out of the bushes. "Yep, I got the whole thing on film."

Max popped out of the bushes, too.

"So, it was you hiding in there?" George asked.

"Yeah," Louie said. "I had to sneak around. How else"—he paused to scratch at his face—"was I going to get **secret footage** of you being a jerk again?"

Mike scratched his arm and held up the camera. "I'd show it to you, but I don't want to get too close. **You stink.**" He turned to Louie and smiled. "The camera was set on *record* this time—I checked."

"Awesome," Louie told him.

Oh man. George was never going to be able to live *this* down.

"FIELD DAY STINKS!" he shouted.

Chapter 11

Mrs. Kelly and Mrs. McKeon decided it was best for George to leave Field Day early. So while the rest of his team were declared the Field Day winners (Alex had managed to find a white pebble by the shore of the lake), George was on his way home. He stunk **so badly** that his own *mom* made him ride his bike while she followed in the car.

Everywhere George rode, people dived out of the way. Babies in strollers held their noses. Squirrels raced up into trees **when they smelled him coming**!

Not that George blamed them. He would have moved out of his own way, too, if he could have.

At home, George had to take a bath in tomato juice. The juice was thick and pulpy. It got stuck in his hair and between his toes. And the juice didn't even really get rid of the skunk stink. George just wound up smelling like **a tomato-covered skunk**.

Yo, Kevin,
I got sprayed by a skunk today. It smelled so nasty! And the only thing that would get rid of the skunky smell was tomato juice. I had to take a bath in it. My mom poured gallons of tomato juice into the tub, and then I got in . . . I hated it. But I know you would have loved it because you are so crazy about tomatoes.
                    Your pal,
                    George

George knew only one person in the whole world who would have had fun getting rid of the smell of skunk: his friend at his old school, Kevin Camilleri. So George wrote and told him all about it.

George didn't go to school the **next day**. He had to stay home until he smelled **less skunky**. Ordinarily that would have made George happy. Just not *that* day. It was the day he was supposed to hand in his sports tape. But since he was absent, **he was out of luck**. Now Louie was going to get to be the fourth-grade sportscaster, after all. That stunk, too. Alex called George right after school. **"You still smell?"** he asked George.

"Yeah," George admitted. "I wanted to help out Mr. Furstman at the pet store. But when I walked over, even he said I stink too much."

"Wow," Alex said. **"That place smells really nasty. You must reek."**

"It's hard to get rid of this stuff," George told his friend. "I've taken three tomato-juice baths already . . . so I guess Louie can't wait to show the whole school the tape of me getting sprayed, huh?" he asked quietly.

"Oh, you don't have to worry about that," Alex said.

"Isn't he the fourth-grade sportscaster?" George asked.

"No," Alex said. "He hasn't been at school, either. Turns out **there was poison ivy in the woods** where they were hiding. Louie's out until he stops itching. So are Mike and Max."

George smiled. "Awesome!"

"That's cold, dude," Alex said.

"No, I didn't mean it's awesome they have poison ivy," George said. "I meant it's awesome that I still have a chance to be the fourth-grade sportscaster."

"Sorry, dude," Alex said. "They gave the job to someone else."

"Who?" George wondered.

"Julianna," Alex said. "I was at the studio today, learning how to work the cameras, and I saw her audition tape. It was pretty good. She interviewed the teachers about other Field Days, which was a **really smooth move**. Then she talked about how she couldn't wait for baseball season because she could tell from the races that there are some excellent runners in the fourth grade. **She knows a lot about sports.**"

That was the truth. Julianna was easily the best athlete in the fourth grade.

"Julianna will be a good sportscaster," George said. "And maybe I can get her to do a report on skateboarding. I'm practicing some **way-cool, new stunts**."

"You should probably wait," Alex said. "You don't want her to be able to smell your 180 coming before she sees it."

"True," George agreed with a laugh.

A few minutes later, George and Alex hung up. That was when he heard something awful. *Really* **awful.**

His stomach began to grumble. And rumble.

George gulped. Oh no! Was the super burp back again?

He sat there at his desk, waiting for the bing-bonging and ping-ponging to start. But it didn't. There was nothing in George's stomach. In fact, **that was the problem**. George's stomach was rumbling because he was hungry.

"Hey, Mom," he called downstairs, "what's for dinner?"

"Spaghetti and meatballs," his mom answered. **"With tomato sauce."**

Oh man. Now George was going to be tomatoed inside *and* out. Still, he was glad that all he had in his belly right now were hunger pains.

Of course that didn't mean the super burp wouldn't be back. **It could happen any time.** And without any warning. In fact, there was only one thing George could count on when it came to the super burp: When it came, it would cause trouble. And that was *ba-a-ad*!

George Brown, CLASS CLOWN

Wet and Wild!

by Nancy Krulik

illustrated by Aaron Blecha

Grosset & Dunlap
An Imprint of Penguin Group (USA) Inc.

Chapter 1

George Brown stared at his computer screen. Louie had invited him to his birthday party. That was weird. *Really* weird. Because Louie *hated* George

From George's very first day at Edith B. Sugarman Elementary School, Louie had let him know that **they were never going to be friends** . . . *ever.* Louie still sometimes

called George **"New Kid"**—like he couldn't be bothered remembering George's real name.

Louie had also gotten George in trouble with the cafeteria lady—the *big, scary* cafeteria lady—just for **sneezing** in the middle of lunch. Apparently Louie didn't like snot anywhere near his food. He'd also thrown George out of a rock band for no reason except that he could.

No doubt about it, Louie *really* didn't like George. And George *really* didn't like Louie, either. **So they were even**.

Of course, that didn't mean George was

going to miss Louie's party. George might not have liked Louie, but he sure liked water parks.

George didn't want to give Louie a chance to take back his invitation, so he quickly typed an e-mail back saying that he would come.

I'll be at your party. Thanks for inviting me.

—George

George didn't even have time to blink before **a new e-mail flashed on his screen**. It was from Louie.

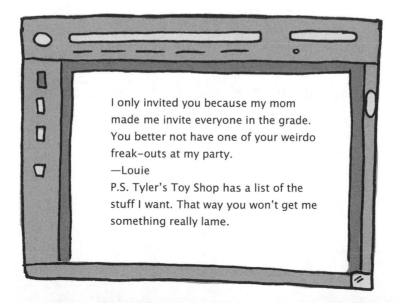

I only invited you because my mom made me invite everyone in the grade. You better not have one of your weirdo freak-outs at my party.
—Louie
P.S. Tyler's Toy Shop has a list of the stuff I want. That way you won't get me something really lame.

Oh brother. *Louie* was the lame one. Still, George understood what Louie meant by "weirdo freak-outs." George *had* been doing a lot of really strange stuff ever since he moved to Beaver Brook.

But it wasn't really his fault. **It was the super burp's fault.**

It had all started on George's first day at Edith B. Sugarman Elementary School. George's family had moved—again. That meant George was the new kid—**again**.

This time, though, George had promised himself that things were going to be different. He was turning over a new leaf. No more pranks. **No more class clown.**

But new George was also **boring George**. At the end of that first day, nobody even seemed to know he existed.

It was like he was *invisible* George.

That night, George's parents took him out for dessert to cheer him up. While they were sitting outside at the ice cream parlor and George was finishing his root beer float, **a shooting star flashed across the sky**. So George made a wish:

I want to make kids laugh—but not get into trouble.

Unfortunately, the star was gone before George could finish the wish. So **only part of it** came true—the first part, about making kids laugh.

A minute later, **George had a funny feeling in his belly**. At first he thought it was because of the root beer float. It was like there were hundreds of tiny bubbles bouncing around in there. They **ping-ponged** their way into his chest and **bing-bonged** their way up into his throat. And then . . .

George let out a big burp. A *huge* burp. A SUPER burp!

The super burp was loud, and it was *magic*.

Suddenly George lost control of his arms and legs. It was like they had minds of their own. His hands grabbed straws and stuck them up his nose **like a walrus**. His feet jumped up on the table and he started dancing the hokey-pokey. Everyone at the ice cream parlor started laughing— **except George's parents**, who were covered in ice cream from the sundaes he had knocked over.

That wasn't the only time the super burp had **burst** its way out of George's belly. There had been plenty of magic

gas attacks
since then.
And every
time the burp
came, trouble
followed.
George never
knew when a burp

would strike or what it would make him
do. Like juggle raw eggs in his classroom
(which **would have been fine** if George
actually knew *how* to juggle).

The super burps even followed George
to the fourth-grade field day. One burp
made George bark like a dog and lick the
principal's hand.

The last thing George wanted was for
the super burp to start bubbling over on
Louie's birthday. George didn't know what
Louie would do if George ruined his party.

And **he didn't really want to find out**.

Chapter 2

"Hi, George. Where are you going?" George's best friend Alex asked him when the boys ran into each other near the park later that Saturday morning.

"Mr. Furstman's pet shop," George said. "I promised I'd be there by noon today." George worked at the pet shop every Saturday. He liked being around the animals. George didn't have a pet. His dad was allergic to just about everything but fish. And fish didn't really count as pets.

Alex looked down at his watch. "It's only eleven," he said.

Alex was the only kid George knew who wore a watch. Most kids just stopped some grown-up and asked what time it was—when they even *cared* what time it was.

But **Alex's watch was definitely cool**. It lit up at night, and you could wear it if you went **deep-sea diving**—not that Alex had ever done that. Alex was more the kind of kid who would wear nose plugs to go underwater in the bathtub. Not that Alex wasn't cool. He just wasn't into doing any kind of sporty stuff. He was more **a science and math kind of guy**.

"I'm going in early because I ran out of stuff to do," George said. "And my mom was yelling at me to turn off the TV. What are you up to?"

"Breaking a world record," Alex said.

George stared at him. *What a weird answer.*

"You know, like in the book," Alex explained.

George knew exactly what Alex was talking about: the *Schminess Book of World Records*. It was filled with pictures of people who had broken **all sorts of records** —like being the person with the longest toenails or plucking a turkey the fastest or eating the most cockroaches in one sitting. George had bought the same book at the school bookfair the week before. **Pretty much all the boys had.**

Alex reached into his pocket and pulled out a plastic bag. Inside was a big, round gray blob.

"What's that?" George asked.

"It's the start of **my world**

record-breaking ABC gum ball," Alex explained.

"What's ABC gum?" George asked him.

"Already been chewed," Alex said. "I'm collecting pieces of chewed gum and sticking them together. **The world record is a wad with a four-foot diameter.** It weighs seventy-seven pounds and twelve ounces. I'm going to keep collecting used gum until this ball is even bigger."

"Wow! Go for it, dude!" George said, **high-fiving** Alex. If Alex really *could* break the world record for collecting ABC gum,

he would get his name and his picture in the *Schminess Book of World Records*. It would be amazing to have a world-famous friend. Almost as amazing as being world-famous himself.

Of course, Alex still had a long way to go. His wad of gum was currently only about the size of a baseball. Still, it must have taken a lot of chewing to even get it to that size.

"You chewed *all* that gum?" George asked.

Alex shook his head. "Nah. Just some of it. **The rest I got other places**—like on the sidewalk or under some desks at school. You'd be surprised where people stick ABC gum. I even found some in a bathroom stall at a diner."

"Come on," George told Alex. He started walking down the street. "Let's hit the newsstand. I'll buy a pack of gum. I'll

chew it up real good and give it all to you."

"You're a good friend, George," Alex said. "Thanks."

"I bet you'll be the **first kid from Beaver Brook** to get in the *Schminess Book of World Records*," George told Alex.

"I don't know," Alex said. "Maybe."

As Alex and George walked to the newsstand, George began to think about what record *he* could break. He didn't want to grow his toenails really long because then he'd have to get all new

shoes, and George hated shoe shopping.
And he wasn't sure he wanted to find
out what it felt like to have a cockroach
crawling down his throat and into his
stomach. **He had eaten worms once—the
burps made him**—and they hadn't tasted
so great.

In fact, the only thing George could
think of that could be world record–worthy
were his burps. And George didn't want to
break that kind of record!

When the boys reached the newsstand,

George counted the change in his pocket to buy **a big pack of Super Bubble Bubble Gum**.

"Dude, there are ten pieces in there," Alex said. "Want me to chew half of them?"

"Sure," George said. He opened the pack of Super Bubble Bubble Gum. Then, suddenly, he felt a fizzy feeling in the bottom of his belly. His eyes **bulged**.

George had felt those fizzies flip-flopping around in his belly before. They could only mean one thing: *The super burp was back, and it wanted to come out and play!*

It had been over a week since his last burp, and it felt like this one was making up for lost time. Already it was ping-ponging its way out of George's belly and bing-bonging its way into his chest.

This could be really *ba-a-ad*!

George had to squelch the belch. Fast!

So **he did the first thing that popped into**

his head. He shoved pieces of bubble gum into his mouth and started chewing as fast as he could. Maybe the gum could block the burp and stop it from getting out of his mouth.

"George, you okay?" Alex asked him.

George didn't answer. He shoved in more gum and kept on chewing. But the super burp was powerful. All the gassy air blew straight into the wad of chewed gum. First it was a small bubble. Then a medium-sized bubble. Then a massive, **gigundo-sized** bubble that was as big as George's head.

"Whoa! This could be a record-breaking bubble!" Alex said.

And then . . .

Whoosh! George felt the air rush right out of his belly. It was like someone had popped a bubble gum bubble inside of him. The super burp had disappeared. Hooray!

Pop! Suddenly, the air rushed right out of the massive, gigundo bubble gum bubble. Pieces of bubble gum were stuck all over George's face—his lips, his hair, **even up his nose**.

George picked a huge glob of gum out of his hair and held it out to Alex. "Here. You want this?"

"Um . . . I don't know," Alex said. "I'm not sure if hairy ABC gum counts."

"Yeah," George agreed. He dug his finger up his nose and pulled a glob of gummy, pink gunk from his nostril. "Guess you don't want this, either," he said.

"I better not," Alex answered. "I don't want to take a chance that I could be disqualified."

George had a feeling he was going to be picking gum off his face and hair for the rest of the day. And none of it was going to be part of Alex's ABC gum ball.

What a waste. Stupid super burp.

Chapter 3

On Monday morning, the whole fourth grade was talking about Alex's ABC gum ball.

"I saved you some of my organic spearmint gum," Sage told Alex. She pulled a small plastic bag out of her backpack. "The minute George told me what you were doing, I wanted to help."

Alex shot George a strange look because it was hard to believe that George would tell Sage anything. Sage had a crush on George. **She made him crazy.**

"She was in the pet store buying bird food and heard me telling Mr. Furstman about you," George explained to Alex. "I was talking about the ABC gum ball with *him*. *She* just overheard."

"So many colorful birds came to the feeder in our yard this weekend," Sage told George. She batted her eyelashes up and down and gave him a **big smile**. "You recommended just the right stuff."

George shrugged. "It's the only birdseed Mr. Furstman sells."

"Well, it was still perfect," Sage said.

"I've got three globs of gum for you," Chris told Alex. "My mom said it was gross to save ABC gum, so I kept them under my bed. But **don't worry, I pulled off all the dust bunnies**."

"Thanks," Alex said. He took the globs of gum and stuck them onto his ball.

George was impressed. The ABC

gum ball was definitely bigger. Alex
had added **a lot of gum** since Saturday
morning.

Just then, Louie strutted onto the
playground. His friends, Mike and Max,
were right behind him—like always.
George called them the Echoes.

"I bet you guys are all deciding what
to get me for my birthday," Louie said.
"Don't stop talking just because I'm here.
I already know what's on the list."

"He knows because he wrote the list," Mike said.

"It's a great list," Max added.

Louie smiled. "I hope someone gets me the night-vision goggles," he said. "And I'd really like that **portable popcorn maker**. It's the third item down on my list. You can't miss it."

"Actually, we're talking about Alex," George told Louie. "He's going to break a world record."

"For what? Having the geekiest friends?" Louie asked.

Mike and Max both laughed.

"At least Alex *has* friends," George said.

Mike and Max stopped laughing.

"Louie has friends," Max said.

"Yeah," Mike added. "What are we?"

George started laughing. **"You don't really want me to answer that, do you?"**

Just then, Julianna came over. She walked right past Louie and started talking to Alex. "I want to interview you for my sportscast this morning."

"Why him?" Louie asked. "Alex stinks at sports."

Edith B. Sugarman Elementary School had its own TV station—WEBS TV. Julianna was **the fourth grade's sportscaster**.

"I want to interview Alex about his ABC gum ball," Julianna explained.

"Since when is collecting used gum a sport?" Louie asked.

"Going for a world record means you are competing for a title," Julianna explained. "And sports are all about competition."

George grinned. She had Louie there.

"Alex, now everyone in the school is going to hear about your ABC gum ball," George said. "They're all going to give you their used gum. You'll break the record in no time!"

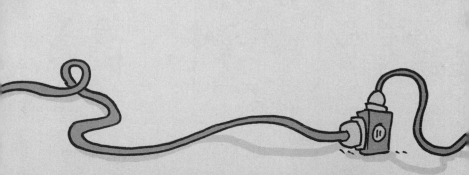

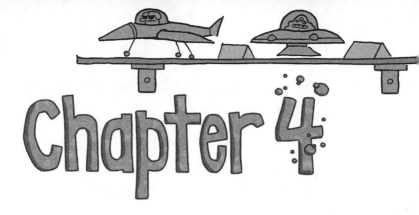

Chapter 4

Even though Louie was a jerk, George still had to buy him a birthday present. So George and his mother went to Tyler's Toy Shop right after school. Alex came with them.

"Louie's list is really long," Alex said. **He held up the two-page printout** Mr. Tyler had given them. "How many presents does he think he's going to get?"

George shrugged. "I guess he's giving everybody a choice."

George's mom picked up an art kit. "What about this?"

Alex shook his head. "Nope. Not on the list."

George stopped in front of a purple-and-green striped basketball. "Is this on the list?"

Alex nodded.

"Maybe I'll get it," George said.

Alex thought for a second. "Bad move," he said. "Louie will use it for **killer ball**. Basketballs are really hard. And that game hurts enough already."

No kidding. Killer ball was a game Louie made up. It was a lot like dodgeball, only meaner. "So what about a deluxe rocket kit?" George said. He picked up the box and read the back. "It says that it is air-powered and can shoot up to two hundred feet in the air."

George's mom looked at the price tag. "It's awfully expensive."

"What if we split it?" Alex suggested.

Before George could ask his mom, he suddenly felt something strange brewing way down in his belly. It was fizzing and whizzing around.

George knew that what he was dealing with wasn't air powered. **It was _gas_ powered.** And no way was it on Louie's list.

The super burp was back! Already it had ping-ponged its way out of George's belly and was bing-bonging up into his chest.

The burp was ready to blast off. And this time it was not going to be stopped. Before George could do anything, the burp ping-ponged right up George's throat, zigzagged its way between his teeth, made its way to his lips, and . . .

"George!" his mom shouted.

"Whoa, dude!" Alex said.

It was the loudest burp anyone had ever heard. It practically broke the sound barrier. Alex was covering both his ears.

Suddenly, George felt his feet running over to the bikes in the back of the store.

"Where are you going?" he heard his mom call.

He wasn't making his feet move. They were doing it all on their own. **It was like George was an old-fashioned puppet and someone else was pulling the strings.** He was heading to the bicycle aisle in the store.

George felt his rear end land—*thud!*—on the seat of a little red-and-white tricycle. The next thing he knew, he was pedaling the trike all around the store.

"Wheeeeee!" George shouted.

George didn't want to ride a baby bike. He really didn't. But George wasn't in the driver's seat now. The burp was.

"George!" his mother shouted. "Get off that, *now*."

Alex was shaking his head and laughing.

George wanted to get off the tricycle.

But his rear end didn't. It felt like it was superglued to the seat.

"*Whee!* Here I come!" George shouted.

Honk! Honk! Suddenly, George's hands began squeezing the big horn on the handlebars. *Honk! Honk!*

"Young man!" a woman in a green floppy hat cried as she leaped out of the way. "You almost ran over my foot!"

"Stop that at once!" Mr. Tyler shouted at George.

Instead, George rode around the lady in a circle. "Beep! Beep! Watch out! I just got my driver's license."

"I'll get my son's birthday gifts another time," the woman with the green floppy hat told Mr. Tyler. **"It's dangerous in here."** Then she raced out of the shop.

"You're scaring away the customers!" Mr. Tyler shouted at George.

The tricycle had now reached the front of the toy store. George's butt

suddenly got unstuck from the tricycle seat. His legs jumped off the trike. George waited to hear the *whoosh* sound that meant the burp was over. But it didn't come. The next thing he knew, George was climbing into the storefront window where there was a huge display of wooden paddleball toys.

George's hands grabbed two paddleball toys. His hands started paddling the balls between George's legs and over his head. They paddled front. They paddled back. George had never been very good at this before. **But now he was a whiz**.

People walking outside on the street stopped to watch him.

The crowd outside was growing. A few little kids were cheering. **The yellow-haired woman in the green sun hat** was staring at George now. She looked so shocked that her eyes were bugging right out of her head.

"George!" Alex shouted. "Are you going for the world paddling record?"

"No. He's not," George's mom said. "GEORGE! Stop that!"

But George's hands kept paddling. They paddled up. They paddled down. They . . . *CRASH!* They paddled right into the display of paddleball toys and knocked it to ground.

Whoosh! Just then **George felt something go pop** in the bottom of his belly. It was like the air just rushed out of him.

The super burp was gone.

George was sitting in the middle of a pile of paddleball toys. He opened his mouth to say, "I'm sorry." And that's exactly what came out.

Mr. Tyler was really angry. "Sorry doesn't fix my display, young man," he told George. "You need to leave. Right now."

"But I haven't bought a gift yet," George said.

"You'd better take your business somewhere else," Mr. Tyler told George's mom. He looked down at George and **frowned**. "*Anywhere* else."

Chapter 5

"So, what are you going to do about a present for Louie?" Alex asked George the next day after school. The boys were hanging out in Alex's backyard.

Alex was staring at George in a weird way. It was like he was trying to figure something out, but he couldn't. It made George feel like **he was a puzzle with a missing piece**. It wasn't a very good feeling.

"I got him a rock music CD," George said. "I had to wait in the car while my mom went into the music store to buy it."

"Probably safer that way," Alex said. Alex stood there for a minute. Then, finally, he said, "Ummmm. Look, dude, **did you ever notice** that whenever you let out a massive burp, you get all weird and wacky?"

"What—what do you mean?" George stuttered.

"You know what I mean," Alex said. "It's like something comes over you, and you go nuts."

George gulped. It was no use pretending nothing was wrong. Alex had figured it out. **Sort of.** Maybe Alex would understand. "It's not my fault," George said. "I get . . ."

Oh man. How was George supposed to talk about his super burps? **It would sound crazy.** It *was* crazy!

"You're going to think I'm nuts," George said slowly. "But right after I moved here . . ." George took a deep breath. "Okay, here goes," he said. "My burps aren't normal burps. They're *magic*."

"There's no such thing as magic," Alex told him.

"Yeah, that's what I always thought, too," George said. "But my burps really are magic."

George could tell by the way Alex was wrinkling his forehead that he didn't believe him. It wasn't going to be easy to get a science guy like Alex to believe in magic.

"Are you talking about magic, like a magic trick?" Alex asked.

"No. *Magic* magic. Not trick magic," George told him. George knew all about magic tricks—he put on shows for his parents all the time. **He was the Great Georgini.** But this was different.

"Whenever I have a magic burp, it takes over and makes me do stuff

I don't want to do. Like yesterday at the toy store. The magic burp made me get on that trike."

"You're serious? You're not kidding me?" Alex stared so hard at George it was like he were peering into his brain. It was the same look George's mom had given him that time she tried to figure out who broke her lamp.

George raised both his hands. "Dude, this is the truth."

"So when you exploded the volcano while we were showing our science project . . . ," Alex began.

"The magic burp," George said.

"And when you jumped off the trampoline and got your underpants stuck on the tree branch—"

"With the world's worst wedgie? **Yeah**, that was the burp, too."

"And when you juggled raw eggs, went

after the skunk, and dive-bombed into the principal's lap?"

"Burp. Burp. And more burp," George said.

Alex sat on the ground. **He blinked a few times.** George could see he was trying to wrap his mind around something big—even bigger than the world's biggest wad of gum.

"Wow. Magic burps," Alex said finally. "When did it start?"

"Just a few weeks ago. I was normal before. I swear," George said. "I had a root beer float at Ernie's, and the first one came right after that."

Alex thought about that for a minute.

"There's got to be a cure. But it's going to take a lot of hard work before we find it, that's for sure," he said.

_"We?"_ George asked. "You're going to help me?"

Alex nodded. "Sure. I don't want you to keep getting in trouble."

"Neither do I," George said. He stopped for a minute. "You won't tell anybody, will you? My parents don't even know."

"Your secret is safe," Alex promised.

"You can't even tell Chris," George went on. Chris was George's second best friend in Beaver Brook. "The fewer people who know about this the better."

George smacked himself in the forehead. "Can you imagine if Louie found out?"

"Yeah, that would be bad," Alex agreed. "He'd never stop making fun of you."

"No kidding," George said. "He'd

probably stop calling me New Kid and start calling me Gassy Guy."

Alex thought for a minute. "Tell me again about the first burp?" he asked.

"It happened at Ernie's," George said. "It was right after I drank a root beer float. But I've had **thousands of root beer floats** in my life. This time, though, a shooting star went by, and I made a wish. I think the wish came true but got kind of mixed up."

"And that's what made the magic burps come?" Alex had an "I don't think so" look on his face.

"Yeah," George said.

"Then we need to go back to Ernie's," Alex said.

"No way," George said. "I did the hokey-pokey on a table with straws up my nose the last time I was there."

"We need to check out the scene of the

burp if we're going to find a cure," Alex insisted.

George folded his hands in front of chest. "Uh-uh."

"How about if you wear a disguise?" Alex suggested.

George thought about that for a minute. **"It would have to be a really good disguise."**

Chapter 6

"I better not run into the waitress who served me that root beer float," George said. He felt **sick to his stomach** as they rounded the corner.

"She'll never recognize you," Alex said. George was wearing a baseball cap pulled low over his eyes and a pair of glasses with a fake nose and moustache attached.

They were standing in front of Ernie's.

"Which table were you at?" Alex asked. "We have to sit at the exact same one."

"Outside. Third one from the left," George said.

Alex and George sat down at the table. **A waiter skated over.** "Hi, guys," he said.

"Hi," Alex answered.

"Hello," George said. He tried to disguise his voice so he sounded older.

"Nice 'stache," the waiter said.

"Thanks," George said.

"What are you having?" the waiter asked Alex.

"I'll have a vanilla and chocolate swirly cone," Alex told him.

"And for you, sir?" The waiter turned to George.

"He'll have a root beer float."

"*Ummm* . . . I don't know about that," George said nervously.

"You have to," Alex said under his breath. "We have to figure out what made the *you-know-what* happen."

"Okay," George said. "A root beer float."

"I'll be right back with your orders," the waiter told them as he skated off.

George looked around. "I don't know what you think we're going to find out here."

"I'm not sure," Alex admitted. "But **scientists always replicate** their experiments to see if the same thing happens again."

"Repli-what?" George asked him.

"Repli*cate*," Alex repeated. "It means do something over and over again. So you have to drink a root beer float over again, just the way you did before. We can see if the burp shows up and makes you act weird. Maybe it's **an allergic reaction** to the root beer they serve."

George still wasn't sure. But at least this experiment involved drinking a root beer float. **That used to be his favorite thing in the world.** But he hadn't had one since that bad, *ba-a-ad* night.

While waiting for their order, George reached under the table. "Hey, check it out!" he shouted. He held up a hardened piece of gum. "ABC gum!"

"Awesome," Alex said. He took the gum from George and squished it onto his **ever-growing gum ball**. It was so large now, it bulged out of Alex's backpack.

George reached underneath his chair. There was a piece of gum there, too. "Here's some more," he said excitedly.

"That one's still a little gooey," Alex said. "Must have been just been chewed."

A minute later, Alex's ice cream and George's root beer float arrived.

"Here you go," the waiter said as he placed them on the table. "Enjoy!"

George stared at the root beer float with its scoop of ice cream and whipped cream topping. **It looked so innocent!** But what if the fizzy bing-bonging and ping-ponging started up again?

Alex was examining the root beer float, too. "You know, it looks like they use extra bubbly root beer," he said. "And maybe it's the bubbles in the soda that make you burp."

"Yeah, but even if the root beer has extra strong bubbles, why would they make me do crazy stuff?" George pointed out.

"That's true," Alex said with a shrug. "But we have to start our experiment somewhere. **Drink up!**"

George put his mouth around the straw.

"Wait!" Alex shouted.

George popped the straw right out of his mouth. "What?"

"You have to drink it *exactly* the same way you drank the float that gave you the burp," Alex said. "Otherwise we are not replicating the experiment. Did you drink it fast or slow?"

"Fast," George said. "*Really* fast. I was thirsty."

Alex looked down at his watch. "Okay, go ahead and drink. I'll time how long it takes you."

"Why?" George asked.

"Because we need all the data we

can collect," Alex said. "That's the scientific way!" He looked at his watch. "On your mark. Get set. Go!"

Slurp.

The creamy root beer went through the straw, into George's mouth, and **down into his belly**.

And then he waited for something *ba-a-ad* to happen.

He waited.

And waited.

And waited. But nothing happened.

"Maybe you have to drink it faster,"

Alex suggested. "Forget the straw."

George picked up the glass and took a huge gulp.

Alex started to laugh.

George stopped slurping and looked up. He hadn't felt any fizzing. He hadn't let out so much as a **mini burp**. And he certainly wasn't dancing on tables or doing anything else weird.

"What's so funny?" George asked.

"Your moustache," Alex said. He pointed to the root beer float.

George looked down. The moustache was floating on top of the drink. It looked like **a big, hairy spider floating on a mountain of ice cream**.

George took the moustache out of the glass. He licked all the ice cream off the ends. No point in wasting perfectly good ice cream. Then he finished the float while Alex sucked the last of his ice cream out of the bottom of his cone.

Alex made George wait fifteen minutes to see if a burp came.

Nothing. Absolutely nothing.

By the time the boys finally left Ernie's, Alex had fourteen new wads of ABC gum stuck on his gum ball. But they hadn't figured out how to stop the magical super burp.

You couldn't find the cure for something like that hidden under a tabletop. Super burps were *w-a-a-ay* **too sneaky for that**.

Chapter 7

By the time Louie's birthday party rolled around, George had been **burp-free for four days**. Alex thought maybe drinking the root beer float at Ernie's had cured George. But he wasn't taking any chances.

One day Alex had said, "I have been doing some research. We need to improve your digestion." So he made George curl up in a ball with his legs tucked into his chest and roll around and around, because Alex read somewhere that rolling around makes stomach gas go away.

Another day, Alex had George breathe into a paper bag three times after every meal.

On the other two days, Alex made George do **one hundred sit-ups** to keep his stomach strong so his muscles could hold down the burp. Just in case.

George did what Alex said, but he was scared the magic burps were just lying in wait, ready to pop out at the worst time— like right in the middle of Louie's party.

"I will not burp. I will not burp," George said over and over to himself as he walked to Alex's house on Saturday morning. George's mom had to work at her shop, the Knit Wit craft store, and his dad was at the army base before George even woke up. So Alex's mom was driving them to the party.

"I will not burp. I will not burp," George said again as he rang the doorbell to Alex's house.

"Hi. How does it feel to go ninety-six hours without a single burp?" Alex asked as he opened the door.

"*Shhhhh!*" George said. **He looked around nervously.**

"Relax," Alex said. "My mom's in the laundry room. You can't hear anything over that clunky dryer. And Chris won't be here for fifteen minutes."

George frowned. He felt bad leaving Chris out of his secret, but if Alex really did find a permanent cure soon, there wouldn't be any burping secret to hide anymore.

"I've been doing more research about burping," Alex told George. "Burps are actually caused by gas."

"Tell me something I don't already know," George said. "I feel fizzy gas all the time."

"Yeah, but did you know that the

gas is made in your stomach and your intestines when your body breaks down food into energy?" Alex asked him.

George started laughing.

"What's so funny?" Alex asked.

"Intestines," George said. "It's a funny word."

"Now listen, you can't eat anything at the party," Alex said. "No food. No burp. **Simple.**"

It did sound simple. Except for one thing: It was a party, and a party meant pizza and birthday cake.

But George would give them up if that was the way to keep Pirate Island a belch-free zone.

The banner for Louie's birthday was the first thing George saw when he, Alex, and Chris entered Pirate Island Water Park later that morning. There was no

way anyone could miss it. Alex's mom
told the man at the ticket stand that
the boys were part of the birthday party.
Then they each held out their hand to
get **stamped with an image of a pirate's
head**.

"This place is the best," Chris said.
"The Barracuda Blast log flume is
awesome. My little brother threw up
on it!"

"Drop your loot right in here," Louie said with a smile.

Louie was standing right inside the entrance wearing a giant pirate hat. Max and Mike were standing beside him holding a large laundry bag.

"*Loot* is pirate talk for presents," Max said.

"Yeah," Mike added. "Pirates have their own talk."

Duh, George thought to himself as he put his CD into the bag with the rest of gifts. But he didn't say that. He was being the new, well-behaved George. **Even at the water park.**

"Oh, and there's no gum-chewing in the water park," Louie said. "That means you can't work on breaking your world record today." He gave Alex a nasty grin.

Alex shrugged. "That's okay. I got time."

"This is going to be the best party ever," Louie said. "You can go anywhere you want in the whole park."

Wow! George liked the sound of that.

"Of course, I'm the only one with a golden ticket. My parents paid a whole lot extra. **Like fifty bucks or something.** But it means I automatically go to the front of the line on any ride," Louie continued. He shoved the plastic card that hung from

a rope around his neck in George's face. "You guys all have to wait in line."

Then Louie passed out a map to each of the guests. The map showed pictures of all the attractions in the park. There was a **giant waterslide** nearby and a log flume right next to it. The map also showed three wild water coasters, a rope swing over a river, and a long, rambling creek that circled the whole park.

"Hey, Ma, hurry up!" Louie started yelling. "Everybody's here."

"I'm coming, Loo Loo Poo," Louie's mom shouted.

George turned and spotted a woman rushing over to them. She was balancing trays with paper cones of cotton candy stuck upright.

The woman had yellow hair, and she was wearing a big green sun hat. **There was something familiar about her.**

Oh man. It was the lady who been in Tyler's Toy Shop the day George had had that major burp attack. *Gulp*. **Quickly** George turned his back to her.

"Ma!" Louie grumbled. "I said to hurry up! I want my cotton candy. Did you get me a purple one?"

Oh no! The woman in the hat was Louie's mom! *Double gulp*.

"It's right here, Loo Loo," she said. "And it's the only purple one. **The birthday boy's cotton candy has to be special.**"

Suddenly Louie's mom stopped in her tracks and took a good, hard look at George. **"Don't I know you?"** she asked.

Triple gulp. "Me? No, no. I'm new in town," George said.

Louie's mom continued staring. "Now I recognize you! You're that crazy kid from the toy store. The one who

practically ran me
over. Aren't you
a little old for a
tricycle?"

Busted.

"I'm going to
keep an eye on
you," she told
him.

*I will not
burp . . . I
will not
burp . . .*
George
kept telling himself as **his hand shot out
toward the tray of cotton candy cones**.
But Alex grabbed him before he took one.

"No way, dude," Alex whispered
inGeorge's ear. "Cotton candy is a burp
waiting to happen."

"Oh, right," George said unhappily.

He put his hand down and said **"no thanks"** to Louie's mom.

"Don't you like cotton candy, George?" Sage asked him.

George shook his head. "I don't want to go in the water right after eating. I could . . . uh . . . get a cramp or something."

"You're not going swimming," Louie said. "It's just a slide."

"Sliding," Max said.

"Not swimming," Mike added.

"I heard him the first time," George told Mike and Max. He really had to get out of there. Louie's whole mouth was turning **bright purple** from his cotton candy. It was making George *sooo* hungry.

"Okay, kids," Louie's mom told everyone. "You are free to walk around the park by yourselves and go on any ride you like."

"You guys ready to go on the H2-Oh No

slide?" George asked Chris and Alex.

"Yeah!" Chris and Alex said at the same time.

"Then come on," George said.

"Wait up!" Sage shouted after the boys. "I want to go on the H2-Oh No slide with you!"

Oh man. Was Sage going to be following George around all day long?

"It's a really big slide," George told her. "And it goes really fast."

"That's okay," Sage said, hurrying to keep up as George and his friends raced to the H2-Oh No slide. There was already a big line. Sage stood beside George and smiled in a way that **made him kind of sick to his stomach**.

"You're so brave, George. I bet you're not scared to go on anything! I'll close my eyes and hold on to you. I know you'll keep me safe."

George pretended
not to hear. And
he pretended not to
notice Alex, Chris, and Sage
finishing their cotton candy.
Instead, he waited patiently as
the line snaked up the stairs to the
top of the slide. He was thinking
about how far up he was and how
fun this ride was going to be.

It was a four-lane slide.
**Each path looped around in a
different, crazy direction.**

At the very top, George,
Alex, Chris, and Sage lay down
on their backs. Sage reached for
George's hand.

George did NOT reach
back. Sage was going to have
to **go it alone**.

"Ready?" the pirate at

the top of the slide asked.

"Oh yeah!" George cheered. He was totally ready to slide down the H2-Oh No. **This was gonna be fu-u-un!**

Wheee! The next thing George knew, he was zooming down the slide. Water was splashing all around him. He was zooming over bumps and zigzagging around turns.

"AWESOME!" George shouted out, although nobody could hear him. **He closed his eyes.** It made the ride even scarier!

Splash! George landed in the big pool of water at the bottom of the H2-Oh No slide.

Splash! Alex plunged into the pool right behind George.
Splash! Down came Chris.
Splash! Sage landed last.

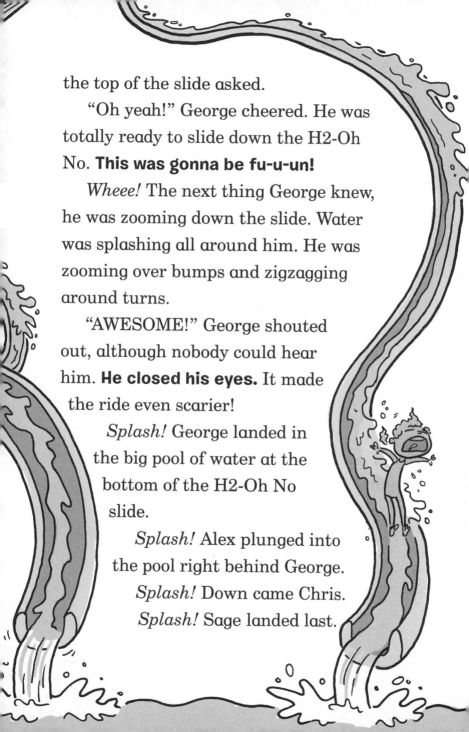

"Yo, Sage, your face is green," George told her as they all climbed out of the pool at the end of the plunge and returned their mats.

Sage didn't answer for a moment. Then she said, **"I think I just threw up a little in my mouth."**

"Cool," Chris said.

"Want to go down again?" Alex asked.

"Maybe let's go for a water coaster." Chris answered.

"Yeah!" George cheered. "How about the one that turns upside-down in the middle?"

Now Sage looked **really** green. "I think I'll go to the arcade. I need to stay on dry land for a while."

"Okay, see you later," George said happily. As she walked away, he added, "All it took to get rid of Sage was a little ABS cotton candy"

"ABS?" Alex asked. "What's that?"

"Already been swallowed," George said. "And then it got thrown up and swallowed a second time."

"Gross, dude," Alex said. But he was laughing, too.

Chapter 8

"Louie, Louie . . . Aye yi yi yi."

The words to the classic rock song blared out from the speakers all around the water park. No way was George—or anybody else—going to forget that it was Louie's birthday.

And then there were the posters. They were everywhere, too. As George, Alex, and Chris floated in their inner tubes around another turn in Castaway Creek,

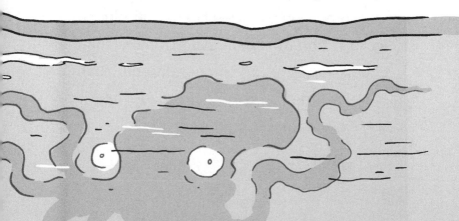

there was Louie's big, goofy face on a poster, saying, *Have You Seen This Guy? If You Do, Wish Him a Happy Birthday!*

HAVE YOU
SEEN THIS GUY?

IF YOU DO, WISH HIM
A HAPPY BIRTHDAY!

Still, George and his pals were having a great time. It was sunny and hot—but not too hot. They were all sitting in their own **bright orange inner tubes**, riding around in a shallow stream of blue water.

Every now and then, the water would start bubbling beneath their rear ends—**on purpose!** It was supposed to make them feel like they were riding in rapids. And then as their tubes went around the bend, a big rush of water would fall from overhead—as if they were going under a giant waterfall.

"Glub! Glub! Glub!" Chris shouted as he opened his mouth and swallowed water from the waterfall.

That looked like fun. George started to open his mouth, too. Suddenly, he got a fizzy feeling in his gut.

George shut his mouth quickly.

Oh no! There was no way. George hadn't had anything to eat or drink. No cotton candy. No root beer. So this couldn't be the super burp.

Or could it? Already bubbles were bouncing around like crazy inside him. Oh yeah! It was **definitely** the super burp. And it wanted out. NOW!

George's eyes opened wide. He waved his arms in Alex's direction, trying to get his buddy's attention. Alex had to help him keep the burp from bursting.

But Alex was too busy paddling his way over toward a pirate cannon on the side of the creek that was shooting cold water at people.

Bing-bong. Ping-pong. The burp was up in George's mouth now. It was zigzagging its way between his teeth and over his tongue.

All of a sudden, Alex spun around. **He'd heard what happened** and started paddling frantically toward George.

Too late. George had already let out a burp so loud it drowned out "Louie Louie" on the loudspeakers.

George opened his mouth to say, "Excuse me." But that's not what came out. Instead, George's mouth shouted, "SHARK!"

Everyone turned to stare at him. One little kid, who was sharing a double tube with his dad, burst out crying.

The burp was in control now. George's legs leaped from his inner tube.

"Dude, no!" Alex shouted.

The lifeguards began blowing their whistles. But if George's ears heard the whistles, they weren't listening. His body was way too busy playing shark attack in Castaway Creek.

George's body dived underwater. He swam underneath Chris's inner tube. Then his fingers pinched Chris's rear end.

George's head popped up from under the water. "Shark attack!" he shouted at Chris.

The lifeguards blew their whistles again. One was shouting through a megaphone, "No fooling around in the water. Stop this instant!"

George the shark wasn't going to stop attacking. He swam around, ducking underwater and pinching rear ends.

"Ouch!" a huge man shouted.

"Shark attack!" George's mouth shouted back.

"Somebody do something about this kid!" a woman in a flowery bathing cap called to the lifeguards.

Suddenly, four lifeguards jumped into the shallow water. They started running toward George.

George's eyes looked left.

His eyes looked right.

There were lifeguards coming from every direction. There was no way out.

And then . . .

Whoosh! Suddenly, George felt something pop in his stomach, like someone had punctured a balloon. All the air rushed out of him. The super burp was gone!

But George was still standing in Castaway Creek. He was surrounded by **angry lifeguards and furious people** in inner tubes.

"Get out of the water—now!" one of the lifeguards told him.

George lowered his head. He grabbed his empty inner tube and climbed out of the creek.

Alex got out, too. He shouted to Chris that they'd meet up with him later.

"Now you see what I'm up against," George said.

"You ate something didn't you?" Alex asked as they returned the tires. **"Come on. Admit it."**

"No! I haven't eaten a thing since we got here," George said.

"It could have been your breakfast,"

Alex said. "Delayed reaction."

They turned a corner to return their tubes, and there was Louie.

"I knew it! **I knew it had to be you!** You're trying to ruin my party!" Louie was screaming so loud his face was turning red.

Louie was standing right next to a poster of himself. A little girl looked at the poster, then at Louie and said, "Hey, happy birthday!"

Louie's face got even redder. "Ma!" he shouted across the creek. "Over here! Now! He's doing it again!"

Louie's mom was in an inner tube in the middle of the creek. At the sound of Louie's voice, she leaped out of her tube and ran through the water, pushing people out of the way with every turn until she reached the exit.

"One more stunt like that, and I'm sending you home," Louie's mom scolded

George. "You're not ruining my darling boy's birthday!"

"So much for the not eating thing," George whispered to Alex a little later.

"I was so sure it would work," Alex said.

"I told you, this is no ordinary burp," George told him.

"No kidding," Alex said. "The burp lasted twenty-two seconds. **I timed it on my watch!**"

"Now do you believe it's magic?" George asked. "It's going to take a lot more than not eating to squelch *these* belches."

"There has to be a scientific reason," Alex insisted. "We just need more time. Some scientists take years to figure stuff out."

Years? **That was way too long.** George didn't want to be burping his way through *college*.

They stopped talking because Chris had just come out of the bathroom and saw them. "Hey, look what I found on the paper towel dispenser," he told Alex. "A big wad of ABC gum."

"I thought people weren't allowed to chew gum here," George said.

"I guess somebody needed to get rid of it," Alex said. He took the wad from Chris.

"Where are you going to keep it?" Chris said.

Alex bent down and stuck the gum to the bottom of his flip-flop. "It'll be safe there."

"So, you guys ready for the Stingray Slam?" Chris asked. "I know I am." Then he looked at George and **shook his head in admiration**. "That shark attack was so funny. Dude, you had me laughing so hard, I swallowed water and started choking."

George didn't answer. It hadn't seemed as funny to him.

Alex checked his map. "The Stingray Slam's not far from here. The line's going to be long. But it sounds like it's worth waiting for." Alex read aloud the description. The Stingray Slam was a way-cool water coaster with lots of twists and turns. But the best part came at the end—a final drop that was three stories tall! You had to be **fifty-one inches** to ride on it. George would just make it!

He only hoped he could leave the super burp behind.

Chapter 9

"This ride was amazing. I've been on it twice already," Julianna told George, Chris, and Alex as the boys approached the Stingray Slam. "You're going to get soaked." **She shook her wet hair.** Water dripped all over George and his friends.

"Whoa! Check it out!" Chris exclaimed.

The Stingray Slam was definitely impressive.

It looked like a regular roller coaster with **cars that looked like manta rays**. But the tracks were all filled with water. Lots of water.

George looked over to his left. There was another poster with Louie's goofy, smiling face on it.

But on this one, somebody had drawn **bunny ears and a moustache** on Louie's face. *Hilarious!*

HAVE YOU SEEN THIS GUY?

IF YOU DO, WISH HIM A HAPPY BIRTHDAY!

"Who did you go on the Stingray Slam with?" Alex asked Julianna.

"Sage was supposed to go with me," Julianna explained. "But when we got to the front of the line, **she wimped out.**"

"You want to do it again with us?" he asked her.

"Sure," Julianna said. "I'd go on this a million times."

A few moments later, George, Alex, Julianna, and Chris were ready to get into the first car of the Stingray Slam. Each car had fins on the sides that looked like manta ray fins.

George was so excited, he didn't even care that at the last minute **Louie flashed his golden pass** so that he, Max, and Mike could push ahead of them in line. They piled into the first car.

George and his pals got into the next car. Everyone waited until all the cars were filled.

"Let's get going!" Louie shouted at the guy running the ride.

"I'm not so sure about this," Max said, looking at the drop.

"Me either," Mike added.

"Yes, you are," Louie told them. "You guys are totally psyched."

"Oh, yeah, right," Max said. "I'm psyched."

"Me too," Mike agreed. "I was so psyched I forgot I was psyched."

"All right, everybody, hold on tight," the guy running the ride said.

And **they were off**!

The water coaster boat started out slowly, climbing up, up, up through the river of water. Then without any warning, it twisted to the right.

Splash! A big shower of water came sloshing into the boat. It hit George in the face.

"Oh yeah!" George shouted excitedly. "I didn't see that one coming!"

"Whee!" Everyone shouted as the car tipped over and whooshed around a bend.

In the car ahead, Louie threw his hands up in the air. George started to do that, too. But then, suddenly, he felt a weird fizzy feeling in his belly.

Oh no! **Not again!** It couldn't be. Not the super burp.

But it *was* the super burp. And it was already starting to bing-bong its way out of George's stomach and into his chest.

This just wasn't fair! How many burps could one guy take?

If George started acting all weird, Louie would never let him live it down.

Wait! **Forget Louie.** If the burp came now, who knew what it would make George do? His life might be in danger!

There was no way George was letting this burp burst out. It was a battle between boy and burp. And this time the boy was going to win!

Quickly, George shoved his fist in his

mouth like a stopper in a bottle. The burp pushed against his fingers. It really wanted to come out.

"Here comes the drop!" Louie shouted. He raised his arms way up in the air.

"*WHOOAAAA!!!*" everyone shouted.

George kept his fist shoved in his mouth. His stomach went up. It went down. The burp pushed harder and harder against his fist.

Splash! As the car hit the water below, a huge wave of water washed over George and his friends. And then . . .

Whoosh! Suddenly, George felt something pop in his stomach like

someone had stuck a pin into a balloon.
All the air just rushed out of him. Yay!
George had squelched the belch!

"That was so much fun!" Alex said as
they climbed out of their manta ray cars.

"Wait until you see the pictures,"
Julianna told him.

"What pictures?" Chris asked.

"Didn't you see **that flash** as we hit
the big drop?" Louie asked. "There was
a camera. When we get to the end of
this ramp, the photo will be up on a big
screen. I can't wait to see mine. I had my
hands in the air the whole time."

As they got closer to the ramp, George
heard one kid saying, "Look at that guy."

"Must be talking about me," Louie
said. "I bet I'm the only kid in the world
brave enough not to hold on."

"Look, there he is now," the girl said.
She pointed in Louie's direction.

"See?" Louie said.

But the girl ran up to George. **"Make your blowfish face again,"** she asked him.

Huh? What was she talking about?

Then George looked up at the screen. There was the photo of Louie with his hands high in the air. Max was crouched down low in his seat. Mike was covering his eyes.

There were photos of Alex, Julianna, and Chris. They were all holding on tightly to the bars and laughing.

And then there was George, with his fist shoved in his throat and his cheeks puffed out **really wide** while he tried to keep the burp from bursting.

He *did* look like a puffy-cheeked, buggy-eyed blowfish.

And the burp had stayed right where it belonged. In George's belly. Now if he could only keep it there for the rest of the day.

Chapter 10

"Will all of Louie's birthday guests please report to Barnacle Barnie's Pizzeria. It's time for lunch!"

George's ears perked up when he heard the announcement coming over the loudspeaker. "I'm eating. I don't care what you say," he whispered to Alex.

Alex shrugged. **"Whatever."**

"Why wouldn't you be eating pizza?" Chris asked.

George looked at the ground. He really hated keeping secrets. Especially from a friend. And now he wasn't sure how he was going to explain this.

"George is . . . um . . . He's trying to break a record," Alex said finally.

"What kind of record?" Chris asked.

"For . . . um . . . the person who goes the longest without eating pizza," Alex told him.

Chris shook his head. "What kind of record is that?" he asked. "That's no fun."

"It's a record that's easy to break," George told him. "There's hardly any competition. But I'm too hungry. I bet I could eat a whole pizza right now."

The boys could smell the pizza before they even walked into Barnacle Barnie's. **It was overwhelming.**

"You guys are all wet," Louie said as George, Alex, and Chris walked into the restaurant.

"It's a water park," George reminded him. "People get wet here."

"Which is why we have towels," Louie's

mother told him. She handed each of the boys a bright orange towel that said *Happy Birthday, Louie!* on it. "You can keep them. They're party favors."

George didn't know why anyone would want a towel with Louie's name on it—other than Louie, of course. But he took the towel, anyway.

"And don't drip on my presents," Louie warned.

"Yo, Louie," Mike called out from a table near the front of the restaurant. "Sit with us."

"Yeah," Max added. "We saved you a seat."

As Louie went off to sit with Max and Mike, George sniffed at the air. *Man, that pizza smells good.*

Just then, Louie's mother walked over to George. "Just remember," she said. "I'm watching you."

George frowned. **Grown-ups always seemed to be watching him.**

"Hey, Mom," Louie called. "Should I open my presents now?"

"I'm coming, Louie," his mom called. Before walking away, she turned around. She pointed to her eyes with two fingers. Then she pointed to George.

He knew what that meant. "You're watching me," George muttered under his breath. "I get it."

A waiter had just set a pie down at their table when suddenly George jumped up. He had to get out of Barnacle Barnie's Pizzeria fast. The fizzy feeling was brewing in his belly.

What if a burp exploded right in the middle of Louie's pizza party? That would be *ba-a-ad*!

"I've got to get out of here," George mumbled to his friends. He was afraid to open his mouth too wide. The super burp was already ping-ponging its way out of his belly and bing-bonging up into his ribs.

"Dude, not the **you-know-what**!" Alex cried. "*Again?*"

But it *was* the you-know-what. *Big time.* George leaped out of his chair and ran for the door.

The minute he got outside, George looked around for some place to hide. He didn't want to **freak out** in public again.

There! On his left! A door!

George had no idea where the door led. He didn't really care. Wherever it was, it wasn't Louie's party. Quickly, he turned the knob, walked inside, and . . .

B·U·U·U·R·P!

George let out a super duper, mighty, mega super burp! It was so loud that everyone in the room turned and stared.

About ten little kids were singing happy birthday to **a boy named**

Will. *Uh oh!* George had just walked into another birthday party.

The next thing George knew, his hands grabbed a long, skinny balloon from the table. Then they started swinging the balloon around like a pirate sword!

"Who are you?" a little kid asked.

George opened his mouth to say, "George Brown." But that's not what came out. Instead, his mouth said. "**Ahoy, mateys!** Captain Long *George* Silver has arrived! *Aargh!*"

"You're late. The other pirates are already here," Will, the birthday boy, said. "See?"

George's eyes looked across the table. Sure enough, there were two waiters in pirate costumes.

"Get out of here, kid," one of them said to George.

George wanted to. He really did. But George wasn't in charge now. The super burp was.

One of the waiters tried to push George out of the room. But George's legs weren't going to let that happen. They jumped up and wrapped themselves around the waiter's back.

"Shiver me timbers!" George's mouth shouted out. "I've got me a prisoner!"

George's hands waved his balloon sword in the air.

"He's funny!" Will shouted.

"Aargh!" George screamed.

Suddenly, all the little kids were grabbing balloons and waving them like swords.

"Aargh!" the kids shouted.

"Aargh!" George's mouth answered.

"Please, children, sit down," Will's parents kept saying.

The waiter tried to wiggle George off of his back. But George's legs held tight.

"Get off me!" the waiter shouted.

And amazingly, that's just what George's body did. His legs let go, and George jumped from the waiter's back . . . **onto the table**.

"Yo ho!" George's mouth shouted out. "Take that! And that! And THAT!"

George was having a duel—with an imaginary pirate.

"Get down from there!" the birthday boy's mom yelled at George.

"Out of my way!" George said. "I'm dueling on the poop deck!"

"Poop deck!" Will giggled. "That's funny."

"I need to make a poop," another kid said.

"Yo ho! Yo ho!" George shouted as he dueled his way down the long table. Cups and plates went flying.

"Watch the cake!" the birthday boy's dad shouted. He raced over and grabbed the cake before George could step in it.

Then the two waiters grabbed George.

"Aargh!" George shouted as he was dragged off the table. He waved his balloon sword and . . . *whoosh*! George felt something pop in his belly.

The super burp was gone.

But George was still there. He opened his mouth to say, "I'm sorry." And that's exactly what came out.

"Sorry doesn't cut it, kid," a waiter said.

"Look at this mess," Will's mother said. "What kind of person ruins a four-year-old's birthday?"

A person with a stupid super burp following him everywhere. **That's who.**

"I'm really sorry," George said. "But it wasn't . . ." George shut his mouth. What could he say? It wasn't me? It was the super burp? Nah. That would never work.

"I still gotta poop," one of the little kids said.

"Happy Birthday," George said to Will.

"Thanks," Will said. "You were funny!"

George smiled. At least the super burp hadn't ruined *everything*.

For once.

Chapter 11

"Yo, where you been?" Chris asked as he and Alex walked out of Barnacle Barnie's a little while later. "You missed lunch."

"I . . . um . . . I had to go to the bathroom," George said. Then he turned to Alex and mouthed the word *burp*.

"We have time for one more ride," Chris said. "You up for the Tunnel of Terror?"

"Definitely," George said. "The map says that it's the scariest water ride in the

whole park. It's not recommended for **children under seven**."

"Yeah, you slide through a tunnel so **it's completely dark inside**. You can't see a thing. You don't know which way you're turning, or when the end of the slide is coming."

"Sounds scary," Alex said. "Let's go!"

"Right behind you!" George told him. "I can't wait!"

But they all had to wait. The Tunnel of Terror wasn't just the scariest water slide at Pirate Island, it was also the most popular. And the line was lo-o-ong. But George didn't care. He was going on this ride no matter what!

The boys left their flip-flops in the cubbies at the bottom of the staircase that led to the top of the slide. Then **they began their long climb**.

"It sure is hot out here," Chris said. He wiped a big glob of sweat from his forehead.

"How's the ABC gum on the bottom of your flip-flops doing?" George asked Alex.

"I had to get rid of some of it, because it was making my shoes stick to the ground," Alex said. "But **a couple of nice big blobs** are still there. I'm going to be able to add a few layers to the gum ball when I get home."

"Awesome," George said.

"Check it out," Chris said. "We're almost at the top."

George's heart was pumping so hard, he thought it was going to burst out of his chest, slide down the Tunnel of Terror, and explode at the bottom in a bloody mess!

"Yay! We're next," George told his friends.

"NOT SO FAST!"

Just then, Louie, Max, and Mike pushed past them on the staircase. **They hadn't been waiting in line.** But here they were.

"It's my birthday," Louie told George. "And I have a golden ticket! That means I don't have to wait. I can go ahead of you."

"But we've been waiting in line for like half an hour," George said.

"Who cares?" Louie told him. "I've been waiting *all year* for my birthday! And you're lucky you weren't kicked out of the park. So just stuff it."

And with that, he pushed right in front of George. Max and Mike pushed ahead, too.

"Hey! It's not *your* birthday," George told them. "And you don't have golden tickets."

"We're with Louie," Max said.

"Yeah, **we're with Louie**," Mike agreed.

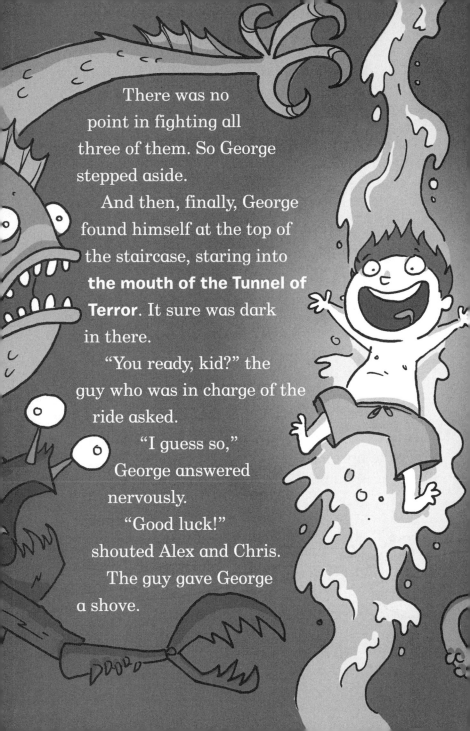

There was no point in fighting all three of them. So George stepped aside.

And then, finally, George found himself at the top of the staircase, staring into **the mouth of the Tunnel of Terror**. It sure was dark in there.

"You ready, kid?" the guy who was in charge of the ride asked.

"I guess so," George answered nervously.

"Good luck!" shouted Alex and Chris.

The guy gave George a shove.

Wheeeee! George went sliding into the darkness.

"Aaaaahhhhh!" George shouted. It was scary in there. **Good-scary,** though. The kind of scary you go to water parks for.

George twisted. He turned. He tried to look around, but he couldn't see a thing. He was going so fast it almost felt like his swimming trunks were being ripped off him.

And then, finally, **he raced out into the daylight** and splashed into a giant pool of water.

Before he could even open his eyes, George heard bells ringing everywhere. Lights started to flash. A woman with a big bunch of balloons raced through the water and came up to him.

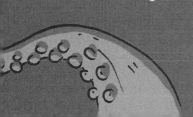

"What did I do?" George asked nervously. He hadn't burped. He hadn't belched. He hadn't even sneezed. So what were all these alarms about?

"Congratulations!" The woman with the balloons shouted to George. "You're the **one millionth park guest** to ride the Tunnel of Terror!"

"Wow!" George exclaimed.

"And here's a lifetime free pass to Pirate Island Water Park," she told him.

"No way!" George exclaimed.

"Congratulations," the woman said. "Smile for the camera. You're going to have your picture in the newspaper."

"NOW WAIT JUST A MINUTE!"

Suddenly Louie came racing through the water. "It's *my* birthday! I should be the one getting the lifetime free pass," he said.

"I'm sorry," the lady said. "But this prize is only for the one millionth guest to ride the Tunnel of Terror."

LIFETIME FREE PASS
PIRATE ISLAND
WATER PARK

1,000,000

George laughed. If Louie had **just waited** for George, Alex and Chris to go before him, he would have been the one millionth person.

Louie stared at George. "This is all your fault."

"Yeah," Mike and Max said at the exact same time.

"*My* fault?" George looked at Louie. "You're the one who butted in front."

Louie was really mad now. He started jumping up and down and splashing the water all around. "I should be the winner!" he shouted. "It's my birthday!"

By now, a whole crowd had gathered at the bottom of the Tunnel of Terror. They were all staring at Louie, pointing and laughing. George didn't blame them. Louie was the one having a weirdo freak-out now. And **George was a celebrity**.

Of course, that didn't mean the super burp wasn't going to cause more trouble. **George had a feeling** there would be about **a billion** more belches to squelch. But for now, anyway, he was burp-free. And that was a great feeling.

George Brown, CLASS CLOWN

Help! I'm Stuck in a Giant Nostril!

by Nancy Krulik

illustrated by Aaron Blecha

Grosset & Dunlap
An Imprint of Penguin Group (USA) Inc.

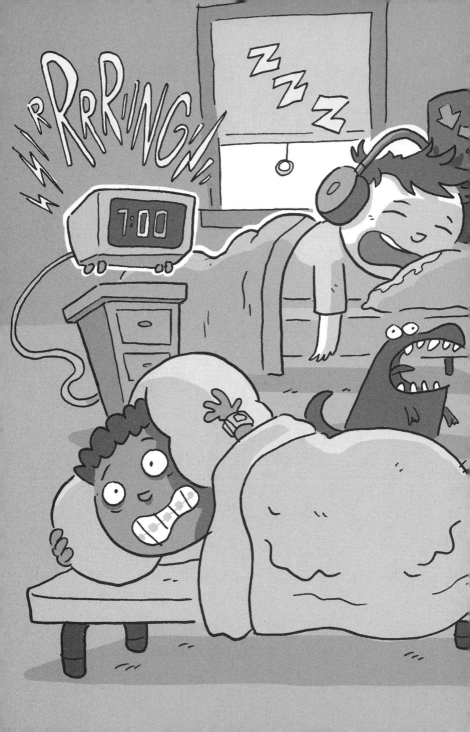

Chapter 1

"You will not burp! You will not burp!"
The whole time George Brown was asleep, his best friend **Alex's voice kept ringing in his ears.** Alex had slept over and right before the boys went to bed, Alex had recorded the message on George's MP3 player.

"You will not burp. You will not burp."

Rrrring! George's alarm clock went off. It was time to get up for school.

"Turn it off . . . too loud," Alex grumbled. He buried his head under his pillow.

George hit the snooze button and rolled over. He *never* got up the first time the alarm clock rang.

Snore. George's nose buzzed.

"You will not burp. You will not burp," Alex's voice repeated over and over.

Rrrring! **The alarm clock sounded** again.

"Boys, are you up?" George's mother shouted from downstairs.

"Yes, ma'am," Alex called back to her. He sat up in his bed and rubbed his eyes.

Okay, now George *really* had to get up. He kicked off the covers and took off the headphones.

"How do you feel?" Alex asked him. "Any **bubbles** in your belly?"

George looked at Alex in the cot that was across the room. George wasn't usually allowed to have **sleepovers on school nights**, but Alex's parents had gone out of town. It was almost like having a brother—for one night, anyway. George sat very still and waited for his tummy to start rumbling.

"Nope," George said happily. "All quiet down there."

"That's a good sign," Alex said. "When I read in that science magazine about **planting ideas in people's heads** while they were sleeping, I figured maybe it would work on your burps."

George frowned when Alex said the word *burp*. George had wanted to keep his burping a secret. But Alex was smart. He'd figured out that George was hiding something. Something really, really awful—**a magical super burp**.

Alex was good at keeping secrets, so he was still the only person besides George who knew about George's problem. And lucky for George, Alex liked solving problems. The super burp was the worst thing that had happened to him since he'd moved to Beaver Brook. It was the worst thing in his whole life.

It all started on George's first day at
Edith B. Sugarman Elementary School.
George's dad was in the army, and his
family moved around a lot. So there always
seemed to be some new school where he was
the new kid.

But this time, George had promised
himself that things were going to be
different. He was turning over a new leaf.

No more pranks. No more class clown. He wasn't going to get into any trouble anymore, like he had at all his old schools. He was going to raise his hand before he spoke. And he wasn't going to make funny faces or goof on his teachers behind their backs.

That last promise had been really hard for George to keep. Especially because his teacher, Mrs. Kelly, looked a little like a totem pole and did weird things like yodel and dance **the hula** right in the middle of class.

At the end of his first day, George had managed to stay out of trouble. Not only had he not been sent to the principal's office, he didn't even know who the principal was!

But you didn't have to be a math whiz like Alex to figure out how many friends being a well-behaved, not-so-funny kid will get you. Zero. Zilch. *None.*

That night, George's parents took him out to Ernie's Ice Cream Emporium. While they were sitting outside and George was finishing his root beer float, a shooting star flashed across the sky. So **George made a wish**.

I want to make kids laugh—but not get into trouble.

Unfortunately, **the star was gone** before George could finish the wish. So only half came true—the first half.

A minute later, George had a funny feeling in his belly. It was like there were hundreds of tiny bubbles bouncing around in there. The bubbles bounced up and down and all around. They **ping-ponged** their way into his chest and **bing-bonged** their way up into his throat. And then . . .

George let out a big burp. A *huge* burp. A SUPER burp!

The super burp was loud, and it was *magic*.

Suddenly George lost control of his

arms and legs.
It was like they
had minds of
their own. His
hands grabbed
straws and stuck
them up his nose
like a walrus. His
feet jumped up
on the table and
started dancing
the **hokey pokey**.
Everyone at Ernie's

Ice Cream Emporium started laughing—
except George's parents, who were covered
in ice cream from the sundaes he had
knocked over.

The magical super burps came back lots
of times after that. And every time a burp
came, it brought trouble with it. Like the
time it forced him to juggle raw eggs in his

classroom (which wouldn't have been so
bad if George knew *how* to juggle).

Or the time he'd burped in the middle
of a toy store and knocked down a whole
display of paddle ball games—right in
the window. A big crowd gathered around
just in time to see him get **kicked out** of
the store!

And who could forget the school talent show? The super burp burst out right in the middle of George's performance. It made him **dive-bomb off the stage**—and into the principal's lap! George definitely knew the principal now. He'd spent a whole lot of time sitting in her office after that one.

Most of the people at Edith B. Sugarman Elementary School just thought George was **clowning around** all the time. Only Alex knew the truth. And he wanted to help.

"Boys, it's **oh-seven hundred hours**,"
George's dad called from the kitchen.
"Better get a move on. Chow's almost
ready."

Alex gave George a funny look. "What
did he say?"

George laughed. "That's army talk for
'it's seven o'clock, and you'd better hurry
because breakfast is almost ready.'"

"Great, and remember," Alex said as they finished getting dressed, "you will not burp. **You will not burp.** You will not burp."

Chapter 2

"I've never had waffles shaped like spaceships before," Alex told George. The boys were sitting in the kitchen while George's parents got ready for work.

"My dad gets them at the PX," George said.

"What's a PX?" Alex asked.

"It's a giant store on the army base," George said. "They have everything." He poured some maple syrup on his waffles.

George was about to take a bite. But before he could open his mouth, he felt **something weird and wild** bubbling around in his belly.

Oh no! Could the super burp be back?

George shut his mouth tight and tried to keep the burp from slipping out.

But the super burp wasn't going to be stopped by two little lips. Already it was bing-bonging its way around George's kidneys and ping-ponging over his liver. Then it zigzagged around George's teeth and . . .

 BUUU-R-P!

George let out a killer burp! It was so loud an alien in outer space could have heard it on his spaceship.

"Oh no!" Alex groaned. "Not again."

Yes, again. **The super burp was out, and it really wanted to play.** Before George knew what was happening, his hands grabbed one of the waffles.

"Heads up!" George's mouth shouted. Then his hands flung the waffle across the table like it was a Frisbee.

Alex ducked. The waffle missed his head. But **a glob of syrup** landed right in the middle of his forehead.

The waffle hit the wall. Ooey, gooey maple syrup splattered all over the place.

"Dude!" Alex shouted. "What are you doing?"

George wasn't doing anything. The super burp was in charge now. It was as if George was an old-fashioned puppet and the burp was pulling his strings.

"Incoming spaceship!" George's mouth shouted as his hands grabbed the waffle from Alex's plate and winged it across the room.

"Boys?" George's mom called from the other room. **"What's going on in there?"**

"N-n-nothing," Alex called back quickly. Then he whispered to George, "Cut it out."

But George *couldn't* cut it out. His hands reached out and grabbed two forks. Then they started playing the drums on the glasses and the plates.

Clink. Clank. Clink. Clank. Crash!

Oops. One of the plates fell off the table and broke into about a gazillion pieces.

"George, did you remember to brush your teeth?" his mom called from the other room.

"Yeah!" George's mouth shouted back. "But I forgot to gargle!" And with that he grabbed a glass of orange juice and poured it into his mouth. Then he gargled the juice straight up into the air—**like a giant George juice fountain**.

Whoosh! Suddenly George felt something pop in the bottom of his belly. It was like

someone had punctured a balloon. **All the air rushed out of him.** The super burp was gone.

But George was still there. And so was the giant mess the super burp had left. There were waffles, syrup, juice, and pieces of the cracked plate all over the kitchen. Alex wiped the glob of syrup off his face and

looked around. "That was a bad one," he said quietly.

George nodded.

"What happened in here?" George's dad asked as he walked into the kitchen. He looked mad.

George didn't know how to answer. He couldn't just say that a super burp made him fling waffles, break a plate, and gargle orange juice.

Alex didn't say anything, either. He looked too scared to even talk.

Besides, George's dad didn't wait for an answer. He handed George a sponge and gave Alex a mop.

"You two are on KP duty," George's dad told the boys. Then he turned and stormed out of the room.

"That means cleanup duty," George told Alex.

"I figured," Alex said. He started swishing the mop around the floor.

"Sorry about this," George said as he wiped some syrup from the wall. "It's the stupid super burp."

"I know," Alex said. "I really hoped that MP3 thing would work. It seemed so simple."

George frowned. Maybe that was the problem. It was going to take something a lot tougher than an MP3 player to squelch that belch once and for all.

"Well, look on the bright side," Alex said.

George gave him a strange look. "*What* bright side?"

"You've already burped," Alex explained. "So maybe you'll be **burp-free** the rest of the day."

George could only hope Alex was right. Because burping at home was a pain in the neck. But burping at school was just plain embarrassing!

Chapter 3

"My nosey nose smells stinky feet. My tingly tongue tastes something sweet!" Mrs. Kelly sang as she strummed a weird, squeaky instrument called a zither. It was kind of like a cross between a guitar and a shoe box. "Ouch! Don't touch a stove that's hot. My eyes can see a leopard's spot. Ask me what my ears can do. They hear **a five-senses boogaloo**."

Mrs. Kelly picked up her zither and started dancing around the room while singing her song.

Mrs. Kelly sure was making it hard to be the new and improved George today. His teacher's singing voice was so bad, it would make a dog howl. And as she passed by, her perfume stunk so much, it would make an elephant fold up its trunk and leave. But he didn't say that. He didn't say *anything*.

"That's a special song I wrote about the five senses," Mrs. Kelly told the class as she finished strumming. **"Smell, taste, touch, hearing, and sight."**

Now this was a subject George knew a lot about. So he raised his hand—like a good George should. Mrs. Kelly gave him one of her big, gummy smiles.

"Yes, George," she said.

"Humans aren't the only ones with senses," he said. "I work at Mr. Furstman's pet store sometimes, and I'm learning a lot about animals.

Like, did you know that scientists think that parrots' eyes are so sensitive that they can see more colors than humans can? Or that hamsters like to taste their food before they eat it? And if they don't like it, they'll spit it out?"

Mrs. Kelly gave George an even bigger grin. Now he could see every one of her big teeth. Yellow stuff was stuck between them. Maybe she'd had eggs for breakfast. "That's excellent, George.

Animals do have very strong senses. Like my cat, Fester. She's a finicky eater, too. But that's because cats have fewer taste buds than we humans do."

"My brother, Sam, will eat anything," Louie volunteered. "One time he even ate snails. His taste buds are **very sophisticated**."

"Sam's a great eater," Louie's friend Max said. "I saw him eat once."

"Yeah," Louie's other friend, Mike, added. "Sam can really pig out."

Louie shot Mike a dirty look.

"I mean in a good way," Mike added quickly.

Mrs. Kelly smiled at the class. "We're going to learn all about the five senses up close and personal," she told them. "We're going on a field trip tomorrow!"

"Ooh!" Julianna exclaimed. "Are we going to **the Human Room-In**?"

"Yes, we are!" Mrs. Kelly exclaimed excitedly. "The whole fourth grade is going to the Beaver Brook Science Center to see their special exhibit on the five senses."

"I've been to the Human Room-In," Julianna told the class. "It's really cool. There's a giant trampoline that looks like a big, red tongue."

Wow! George was really excited now. **This sounded cool!**

"My brother, Sam, and I have been to the Beaver Brook Science Center a gazillion times," Louie said. "We have special passes."

George looked over at Alex. **"Here he goes again,"** he whispered. "Brag, brag, brag."

"George, do you have something to add?" Mrs. Kelly asked him.

Oops. George had almost forgotten to be new and improved. "No. I was just saying that having to wait until

tomorrow is a drag, drag, drag."

Phew. Good save.

"We're all excited," Mrs. Kelly agreed. She gave Louie a gummy smile. "Did you want to tell us something else about the science center?" she asked him.

"We have to make a stop in my new room," Louie told her. "My family gave **a ton of money** to the museum, so they named a room after us."

The kids all looked at him strangely. Who had their own room in a museum?

"It's the Farley Family Fungus Room," Louie explained. "My dad once had **a really bad case of athlete's foot**. His feet got all crackly and red. Finally, this one doctor, Dr. Pedis, got rid of it for him. So my dad donated this money so people could find out more about fungi."

"We'll definitely go in that room, Louie," Mrs. Kelly said. "I can't wait to see what fungi they've found."

"It's *full* of fungi," Louie assured her.

Louie was bragging again, although

having your own room in a museum was pretty cool. But it wasn't a surprise. Louie was rich. He had lots of things no one else had. And he always made sure everybody knew about them.

That was another way George and Louie were different. **George had something no one else had, too.** Only he never bragged. A burp was something you just

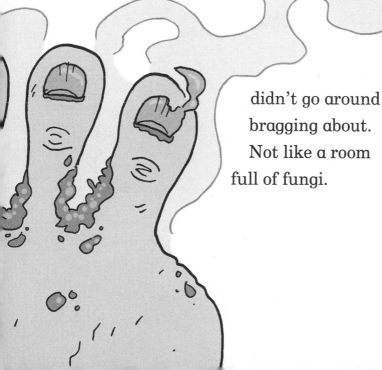

didn't go around bragging about. Not like a room full of fungi.

Chapter 4

"Dude, I can't believe you're going to eat that spaghetti," George said to his friend Chris as they sat with the other fourth-graders during lunch.

"I like spaghetti," Chris told him.

"Me too," George said. "But it's all mushy and covered in gunk."

"It's okay," Chris said. "I don't have to chew as much this way."

George looked at the spaghetti in tomato sauce on his lunch tray. A part of him wanted to shove strands of saucy spaghetti up his nose and let them hang down. They would look like **the world's longest bloody boogers**. That would have cracked up the kids in his old school.

But that was then. This was now. And George wasn't going to stick stuff up his nose anymore. He started eating his canned peaches instead.

"This field trip sounds awesome," Alex said. "The last time I went to the science museum I got to slice up a cow eyeball. It was the size of a Ping-Pong ball."

"**At my old school**, we once went to a natural history museum and someone yanked a bone out of this giant dinosaur and the whole thing collapsed. *Boom!* The guy who worked there burst out crying. It was even in the newspaper!"

Sage shot George a goofy smile and batted her eyelashes up and down. "That sounds like the coolest field trip ever, **Georgie**," she said.

George felt like he was going to puke up his peaches. Why did Sage have to call him that?

Louie overheard George. He poked him in the back. "So what if you went to see some dumb dinosaur on a dumb old field trip from your dumb old school," he said. "Wait until you see the giant mushrooms in the Farley Family Fungus Room. You can look through a microscope and see athlete's foot fungus up close. It's disgusting!"

POKE

"Foot fungus is way cooler than a dinosaur bone," Mike said.

"Yeah, you should see the fungus on my dad's big toe," Max added. "Even at the beach my mom makes him wear socks so she doesn't have to look at it."

George ignored Louie and the Echoes. "You guys want to hang out after school today?" he asked Alex, Chris, and Julianna. "We can go to my house. We can take turns on my skateboard."

"My brother, Sam, bought a superdeluxe skateboard," Louie told George. "It cost two hundred dollars. He did this new trick where he popped way up in the air. Of course, he can only go on it when he's not at baseball practice. You should see him play baseball. He's—"

"We know. We know.

The Yankees can't wait to sign him." George interrupted Louie. Everybody in the fourth grade heard about Sam all the time. How he was president of his class in middle school and how he was captain of the soccer and basketball teams.

"Sam, Sam, Sam," George said to him. "I bet you can't go a whole day without talking about your big brother."

Everyone stopped and stared at George.

"Whoa," Mike and Max said at once.

"Oh yeah?" Louie said. "Well, uh, well . . ." Louie seemed stumped for a minute. But then he said, "I bet you can't go a whole day without talking about your old school."

"Sure, I can," George said. "No problem."

Louie smiled. "Good, **then it's a bet**."

Mike looked at him. "What are you betting?" he asked Louie.

Louie thought for a minute. Then a creepy smiled spread across his face. "Whoever loses has to be **the winner's servant** for a whole day."

"Yeah?" George said. "My mother's been bugging me to clean my room. So *when* you are my servant for the day, be sure to bring dust rags and a broom."

"It'll never happen," Louie told him. "You're going down, Brown."

"Yeah?" George said. "Well, Farley, you're going . . ." George stopped. He couldn't think of anything that rhymed with Farley except barley. That didn't sound bad enough. "You're going to lose," he said finally.

Chapter 5

"Why did you make that bet with Louie?" Julianna asked George that afternoon after school. She, Chris, and Alex were all hanging out on George's front porch. "If you lose, he's going to make you miserable."

George popped a piece of cinnamon gum in his mouth and grinned. "I'm not going to lose the bet," he told Julianna.

"Louie will talk about Sam way before
I talk about **my old you-know-what**. He
can't help himself."

Chris popped a cinnamon gum bubble.
"Louie brags about Sam a lot," he said.

"He brags about *everything*." George
shoved another three sticks of gum in his
mouth and started to chew. Red drool spit

out of the corner of his mouth. It looked kind of like blood.

"Chew the gum really, really well before we add it to the ABC gum ball," Alex told the other kids. "It needs to be sticky. Otherwise it falls off."

Alex was trying to break the record for the biggest already been chewed gum

ball so he could get in the *Schminess Book of World Records*. All his friends were helping him.

George pulled his wad of chewed-up gum out of his mouth and handed it to Alex. Then he grabbed his skateboard and helmet. **"You guys ready to ride?"** he asked.

"Sure!" Julianna said.

"Are you going to show me how to do a 360 kick flip today?" Chris asked. "You said you would."

"Definitely," George agreed. "It's not that hard." He picked up his skateboard

and walked to his driveway. He noticed that his dad had raked up all the leaves in the front yard. There were huge piles everywhere.

George put his skateboard down and snapped on his helmet. The driveway went downhill, and the cement was nice and smooth. **It was a pretty good place to do a 360.**

"Okay, so to do a 360 kick flip," he told his friends, "you put your front foot just

behind the front truck bolt on the board.
Then as you move, begin to wind your body
a little bit, so when you go in the air you are
ready to spin—"

Suddenly, George stopped talking.
Something weird was spinning inside him.
Something awful. And it was all George
could think about.

Bubble. Bubble. **George was in trouble.**

The super burp had stayed inside all through the school day. But now it wanted to come out and play.

George shut his mouth tight. He pushed really hard on his stomach. **He just had to squelch this belch!**

But the burp was strong. Really strong. Already it had bing-bonged its way out of his stomach and ping-ponged its way up into his throat. *Bing-bong. Ping-pong. Bing-bong.*

George let out a burp. A **superpowered**, 360-degree mega burp. It was so loud, it shook the leaves right off the trees!

"Uh-oh . . . ," Alex said
with a gulp. He raced
after George and tried to
tackle him.

But Alex was no match for the
super burp.

Oomph. Alex fell face-first on the
front lawn.

George's legs bent at the knees. His
skateboard sprung up off the ground.

"Cowabunga!" George shouted as he
ollied through the air and landed in the
biggest pile of leaves.

**Red, yellow, and orange leaves flew
everywhere.** Then he headed for the
second-biggest pile. Chris and Julianna
ran up onto the lawn.

"Your dad is going to kill you!"
Julianna shouted.

But the super burp didn't care what kind of trouble George was going to be in. Burps just want to have fun!

George's hands grabbed bunches of leaves and started shoving them down his pants and up his sweater. He stuck a leaf up his nose and another in his ear.

"You look like a scarecrow!" Chris laughed really hard.

That was all George's ears had to hear. He stuck his arms straight out like a scarecrow. Then his mouth began shouting really loudly. "Boo! Are you scared crows? Boo!"

"Caw! Caw!"

At just that moment, two big, black crows flew by. They weren't scared by the George scarecrow at all. One of them landed on his head. The other perched on his arm.

"Caw! Caw!" the crow on George's head cried out.

"Caw! Caw!" George's mouth shouted back.

Now the crows were scared. They took off and flew away—but not before one of them left George a **special present**.

"Whoa!" Alex exclaimed. "Feel that slime dripping on your head? It's crow poop!"

Suddenly . . . *whooosh!* George felt something go pop in the bottom of his belly. It felt like the air had rushed right out of him.

The super burp was gone. **But George was still there**, with leaves stuck in his sweater and crow poop on his head.

Alex raced over to him. "I tried to stop you . . . really I did," he said.

George nodded. "It's not your fault." He looked around at the yard. "I gotta clean up this mess before my dad sees it." The words were barely out of his mouth when his dad pulled up in his car.

"George!" he shouted as he opened the front car door.

The kids all gulped.

"It took me two hours to rake those leaves," George's dad said. He was standing with his hands on his hips and shaking his head. "What happened?"

"It's all my fault, Dad," George said, even though it wasn't. **It was the burp's fault.** "I'm really sorry."

"George—*um*—was trying to be a scarecrow," Chris told him.

George could tell Chris was trying to help. But it wasn't working.

"Why would you want to do that?" George's dad asked.

"Um . . . to scare away crows?" Alex answered hopefully.

"He did it, too," Julianna said. "A couple of crows came by, but they flew off because they were really scared."

"See, Dad?" George asked, pointing to the bird poop on the top of his head.

"Well, George's job isn't to be a scarecrow," his dad said. He went into the garage and came back with a rake. "Your new job is to rake up all these leaves again."

"But, Dad," George pleaded. "I was just about to teach Chris how to do a 360 kick flip."

"Not today, you're not," George's dad told him. "Attention!"

George stood up straight.

"Now start raking," his dad ordered.

"Yes, sir," George said sadly. He started moving the rake around the lawn.

"We'll stay and help," Alex said.

George's dad shook his head.  "George made the mess. He'll clean up the mess."

As George's friends walked off, waving sadly to him, George's dad frowned. "Sometimes I just don't know **what gets into you**, son," he said.

George didn't know what to tell him. After all, it wasn't what got into George that caused all the trouble. It was what burst *out* of him—big, troublemaking burps.

Chapter 6

Bump! Thump! Bump!

"Whoa." George rubbed his rear end as the school bus hit another pothole.

Alex groaned. **"It's like being on a bad roller coaster.** I hope we get to the museum soon."

"At my—" George was about to say how at his old school they took nice buses with seats that reclined and bathrooms in the back. But he stopped himself the minute he saw Louie staring at him.

"What were you going to say?" Louie asked him.

George shook his head. **"Nothing.** I wasn't going to say anything."

Louie frowned, which made George smile for the first time that day. He was in a rotten mood. It had taken him three hours to rake the leaves yesterday, and after that his dad had still made him do his regular chores like taking out all the trash. His arms and legs were really sore. **Yesterday's super burp had really been a pain.**

"What if I burp at the museum?" George said quietly to Alex.

"Maybe we should come up with a signal," Alex suggested. "So if you feel like the you-know-what is about to come out, I can grab you and take you into the bathroom or some other place where you can't get in any trouble. I'll stick close by you."

George wasn't sure there was any place where the super burp couldn't get him into trouble. But it was worth a try.

"How about you **tap your belly**?"
Alex suggested. "It always starts there,
anyway."

George nodded. A tap wasn't the kind
of thing that would look too weird to the
other kids. It might just work.

That made George feel a little better.
But he thought of something that would
make him feel *a lot* better.

"Hey, Louie," George called. "The museum sounds so cool. I know there are a lot of things for **us fourth-graders** to see. But what about older kids? What kind of stuff is there for them?"

"Are you kidding?" Louie asked. "My older bro—" He stopped himself in the middle of the word. "Nice try, George," he said. "But I'm not saying anything."

"Me either," George told him. "In fact, I'm not going to say another word until we get to the museum." And with that, **George zipped his lips**. It was a lot safer that way.

"Here we are!" Louie shouted excitedly as the kids walked into the exhibit. "The Farley Family Fungus Room!"

George looked to his left. There was **a huge sculpture of the entire Farley family**

next to the sign. For a minute, George thought about chewing up a piece of gum and sticking it in Louie's nose so it would look like snot. That would have been pretty funny. But it wasn't something a new and improved George would do. The new and improved George didn't want to

get into any trouble on this field trip.

George and Chris started to walk around the room. They stopped and stared at a big bathtub oozing with mold.

"That's a good reason to never take a bath," George pointed out.

"I bet there's **really nasty fungus** around a toilet bowl, too," Chris said. "Maybe I can put that into my next Toiletman comic. He could be fighting fungus in bathrooms across the world."

"Yeah," George said. "You could call it *Toiletman: Fighting a Fungus among Us!*"

The boys passed by a computer where

Sage and Julianna were playing Find the Fungus.

"What exactly is a fungus, anyway?" George asked Chris. "Is it some sort of plant?"

Chris shrugged. "I thought it was a type of animal."

Mrs. Kelly heard them talking. "Actually fungi aren't animals or plants. They're their own scientific family. Scientists have found at least seventy-five thousand different kinds of fungi. Mold is a fungus. So is yeast."

George looked around for some interesting fungi. But **all he saw were mushrooms**.

"Then why are these here?" George asked out loud. "Aren't mushrooms plants? Like vegetables?"

"Nope. Mushrooms are a kind of fungus," Louie told him. He sounded really proud that he knew that. "And these aren't just any mushrooms. These are some of the **most interesting** mushrooms in the world."

Interesting mushrooms? Those were two words that George didn't think belonged together. Why come all the way to the museum to see mushrooms? They could have stayed in the school cafeteria and taken a tour of the salad bar.

Still, a few of the mushrooms were kind of cool. Especially the giant red one with the little, white blobs all over it.

"I wouldn't want that on my salad," George joked.

"You're not kidding," Alex told him. "According to what it says here, that's an amanita mushroom. It's poisonous. **Two bites could kill a grown man.**"

George put his hands around his throat, tipped his head back, and let his tongue flop out of the side of his mouth. He looked like a guy who'd just been poisoned.

"Hey, don't goof around," Louie said. "Fungi are serious business."

George laughed. **Louie could be such a weirdo.**

"Want to go watch the movie about the life cycle of the yellow brain fungus?" Chris asked George and Alex.

"If you and George want to," Alex said.

George shrugged. He couldn't imagine that a yellow-brained fungus had a very exciting life. So instead he walked over to a diorama where there were 3-D models of people's feet with round, red ringworm fungus. The skin looked all dry and scaly.

"Ringworm is an itchy fungus," Louie told him. "A lot of athletes get it because they walk around barefoot in the locker room and it gets into their feet."

George smiled. "Do you know any athletes who have had ringworm?" he asked **Louie**.

"Sure," Louie said. "Friends of my bro—" He stopped for a minute and shook his head. "Oh no! But you're not

getting me to say what you want me to say. I told you, **you're the one going down, Brown**."

Grrr. George almost had him that time.

Looking at the scaly ringworm feet made George feel **all itchy**. He reached down and scratched his belly.

Suddenly, Alex grabbed his arm and yanked him away from the other kids.

"Outta our way!" Alex said as he pulled George across the room.

"What are you doing?" George shouted.

"This is for your own good," Alex told George as he pushed him into the bathroom.

George rolled through the door and lay sprawled out on the tile floor. "Why are you doing this?" he asked Alex.

"To keep you out of trouble," Alex answered. He stopped and looked curiously at George. "Aren't you going to burp?"

"No," George said as he stood back up.

"But you scratched your belly," Alex told him.

"Because I felt itchy looking at the ringworm," George said. "Besides, the burp signal is *tapping* my belly, **not scratching it**."

"Oh yeah," Alex said. "It's kind of confusing. Sorry."

"How about I tap my belly and rub my head at the same time if I feel the super burp?" George suggested.

Suddenly there was a knock on the door. "Are you boys okay in there?" Mrs. Kelly asked.

Alex opened the door and walked out with George.

"We're fine," Alex said. "Um—I just had to go to the bathroom really bad. And you said we weren't allowed to go anywhere without a buddy. So I grabbed George."

"Oh," Mrs. Kelly said. **"That was very responsible of you, Alex.** Now follow me, boys. We're ready to go into the

Human Room-In. Unless you want to see some more fungi."

George thought about the moldy bathtub, the huge, red mushroom, and the funky feet with ringworm. "Nah. I'm good," he said.

"Me too," Alex said.

George whispered to him, "I'm never asking for mushrooms on pizza again."

NOW LEAVING THE FARLEY FAMILY FUNGUS ROOM

Chapter 7

Lub-dub. Lub-dub. Lub-dub.

The giant heart beat loudly in George's ears as he and the other kids filed one by one up the ramp of the giant heart and through the tricuspid valve.

"You are now traveling the route **real blood corpuscles** take when they go through the heart," a recording said.

"Corpuscle George Brown reporting for duty," George said. He raised his hand in a salute.

"At ease, corpuscle," Julianna said.

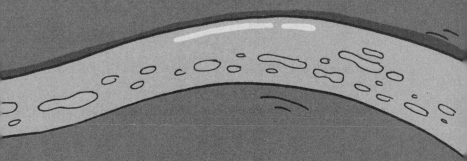

She was right in front of George. "See, I told you this was fun. And it only gets cooler."

Lub-dub. Lub-dub.

Julianna was right. But going through the heart was also a little scary—it was so dark and noisy. **George wondered if his blood got freaked out** every time it went through his heart. It was probably even darker and noisier inside his body. Not just the heartbeat. What about the super burp? It sounded so loud from the outside. He couldn't even imagine what it sounded like *inside*.

"Hey, Julianna," George said. "Do you know where vampires keep their money?"

"No, where?" Julianna called back to him.

"In a blood bank!" George started to laugh. That was a pretty good joke. Not a super burp kind of joke. **Just a normal kid joke.** The kind of joke George always liked to tell when he was a little nervous.

HUMAN

When George emerged from the giant tunnel that was the aorta, he found himself in a different room, **a room as big as the school gym**. It wasn't dark anymore. It was really bright. Kids were running around everywhere. Some were jumping

THE ARMPIT ARCHES

SNOT SLIDE

TONGUE TRAMPOLINE

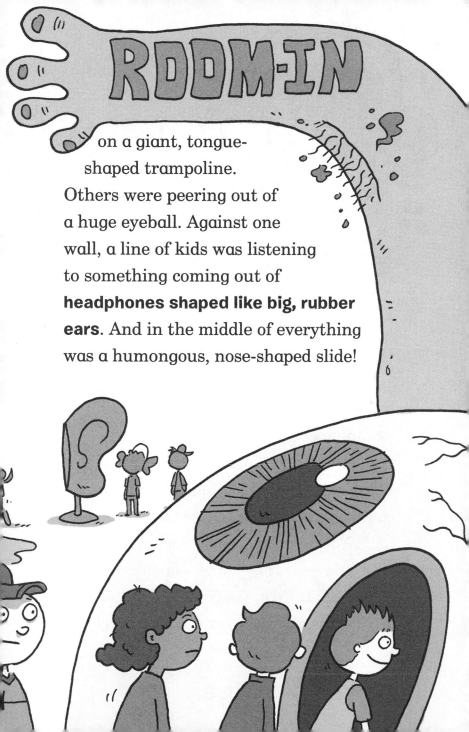

ROOM-IN

on a giant, tongue-shaped trampoline. Others were peering out of a huge eyeball. Against one wall, a line of kids was listening to something coming out of **headphones shaped like big, rubber ears**. And in the middle of everything was a humongous, nose-shaped slide!

There was only one place this could be. George had entered the Human Room-In!

Alex rushed over to the You Are Hear listening booths. He put ear-shaped headphones on and looked like he was bopping up and down to some kind of music. **That looked like fun.** But before George could go over to Alex, Sage called him over.

"Georgie, come here," Sage said. She was standing near the eyeball beneath a sign that read: Do You See What I See?

"Is this a princess or an old witch?" she

asked as she pointed to a poster on the wall.

George looked at the picture. If he squinted his eyes, he saw a young princess. But if he focused really hard on the princess's chin, it became an old lady's giant nose.

"I'm not sure," George said. **He squinted a little harder** to see if he could tell.

"That's why it's called an optical illusion," a museum worker named Meg told him. "You aren't sure what you see. Maybe it's a picture of both!"

"Hey, George, check this out!" Alex shouted suddenly.

George turned around. Alex had left the hearing station. Now he was climbing up on the big, red, tongue-shaped trampoline. That was **the taste station**. George walked over for a closer look.

The trampoline was covered with bumps. A museum guard was explaining that they were supposed to be taste buds. The words *sweet, sour, salty,* and *bitter* were written on the tongue. Right now, Alex was jumping on the front of the tongue trampoline, right on top of the word *sweet*.

"Come on!" Alex called to George.

No way. George
was not getting on
any trampoline.
Not even a cool one
that looked like a
tongue with taste
buds. The last
time he'd been on
a trampoline, he'd
jumped so high
his underwear got
caught on a tree
branch. Man, that
was **the world's
worst wedgie**. His rear
end hurt just thinking
about it.

Instead, George walked over to the
table where Chris and Julianna were
standing. The sign on the table read:
PLEASE TOUCH . . . IF YOU DARE.

There were round holes in the table; you were supposed to stick your hands in them. That way you could feel without seeing **what was lurking underneath the tabletop** in buckets.

"Uh, what's in there?" Chris exclaimed. He yanked his hand out quickly.

That got George's attention.

"Stick your hand in," Julianna told him.

George stuck his hand into the hole. *Oooh.* "Yikes!" he exclaimed. He pulled his hand out.

"Feels like teeth, doesn't it?" a security guard named Don asked him.

George nodded. "Wet teeth. Like ones that just came out of someone's mouth. **I think one of them tried to bite me.**"

"I doubt it," Don said.

"Why?" George asked him.

"Because corn kernels don't bite," Don told him. He pulled out a few kernels to show George.

"I was so sure it was teeth," George said. It was disappointing. Teeth would have been **so much cooler**.

"Don't feel bad," Chris said. "I was sure I was holding an eyeball. But it turned out to be just **a peeled, wet grape**."

"Your senses can play tricks on you," Don said with a smile.

Alex walked over to where George, Julianna, and Chris were standing. He looked up at Don. "Can I ask you something?" Alex asked him.

"That's why I'm here," Don said.

"Does gum really stay in your stomach for seven years if you swallow it?" Alex asked.

Don shook his head. "Nope. That's a myth. You actually don't digest gum at all. After you swallow it, it slides right through you and comes out in **your waste product**."

George laughed. He knew what that meant. "I'm all for helping you find already been chewed gum, dude," he told Alex. "But when it comes to already been pooped gum, you're on your own."

"I'll pass on that, too," Alex said. "No ABC gum for me!"

Just then, out of the corner of his eye, George spotted Louie. He was climbing a tall ladder. The ladder led up to the very top of a giant nose. Max and Mike were right behind him.

"The nose slide is really fun," Don told the kids. "You follow **the path of a sneeze** as you slide through the nose. And every now and then a new smell gets blasted

346

into the nostrils!"

George laughed. "I guess that makes Louie a giant booger!" he said as he watched Louie disappear into the giant nose.

"Max and Mike, too," Chris added. **"That sure is a runny nose!"**

George started laughing. He really wanted to check the slide out. But George stood right where he was and frowned.

Something was happening to him. And it wasn't funny at all!

Chapter 8

Bing-bong! Ping-pong! Bing-bong!
The magical super burp was back.
And it wanted out. NOW!

Boing-bing-boing! The bubbles
were bouncing all around now. Up over
George's kidneys and around his liver.
Ping-pong-ping! **The bubbles danced
their way into George's throat.** They
were headed straight for his lips.

George tapped his belly. He rubbed
his head. He tried to call out to Alex.
But Alex was staring at all the optical
illusions.

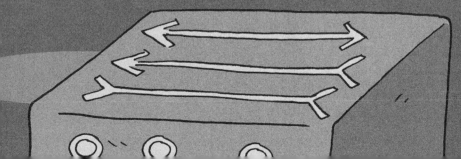

Unfortunately, the super burp was no illusion. It was **the real deal**. And it was on its way out.

George shut his mouth tight. He spun around in circles, trying to force the burp back down like water in a drain.

But the burp was strong. And it was mad that George had beaten it last time. No way was it losing again.

Bing . . . bong . . .

George let out a massive, mega burp! **The loudest burp in the history of burpdom!**

Everyone in the Human Room-In stopped what they were doing. Even the kids with the ear headphones on. They stared at George.

George opened his mouth to say "excuse me." But that's not what came out at all. Instead, George started dancing his way over to the giant nose and singing.

"It's the booger boogie! Everybody do the booger boogie," he sang out. **His rear end wiggled.** "Booger boogie!"

"What is that boy doing?" Meg asked Don.

"I think it's called the booger boogie," Don told her.

"Come on!" George's mouth shouted. "Everybody join in!" His finger shot up into his nose and wiggled all around. "Everybody's doing it, doing it, doing it. Everybody's chewing it, chewing it, chewing it. Thinking it's candy, but it's *snot*!" George's mouth sang out. He could

see Alex trying to rush over to help. But his path was blocked by a **bunch of kids all trying to do the booger boogie with George**.

"George!" Mrs. Kelly warned. "We're at a museum. That song is not appropriate."

"Georgie, you're so funny!" Sage giggled.

"Do the booger boogie!" Chris called out from the top of the giant nose slide. Then he slid down to the ground.

"Do the booger boogie!" Julianna sang from the tongue trampoline.

Max and Mike started to do their own booger boogie. But one look from Louie stopped them cold.

George's feet ran up the giant nose slide. His head poked its way up into one of the giant nostrils.

And then his body started climbing in.

"George!" Mrs. Kelly scolded. "You're not supposed to climb up into the slide. You're supposed to slide down."

But George's body scrambled farther up into the nostril. And then . . .

Whoosh! George felt something pop in the bottom of his belly. It was as if someone had busted a balloon down there. The super burp was gone. But George was still inside the giant nose. And he couldn't get out.

He wiggled to the left. He wiggled to the right. He sucked in his belly. But he was still jammed tight.

"Help! I'm stuck in a giant nostril!" he shouted.

"Ha-ha, kid. Very funny. Now come on out of there," a guard said.

But George wasn't kidding. He was really stuck. His legs were hanging out from the bottom of the giant nose like two long strands of boogers. Well, boogers with sneakers on the ends of them.

Inside the nostril, **tiny, wiry hair things** stuck out all over the place. Again, George tried to twist and wiggle free. But he was still stuck. Even worse, those wiry hair things were tickling his face and arms.

"Cut it out," George shouted. He kicked his legs up and down. "That tickles."

Just then George heard someone outside. It sounded like Louie. "George is freaking out again. I'm sure glad he didn't do this in the Farley Family Fungus Room. You can't freak out around fungus!"

Poof! Just then a blast of air poured into the giant nostril. **Spicy pizza smell filled the whole nose.**

Poof! Another blast of air poured into the nostril. This one didn't smell like pizza. It smelled like stinky gym shoes. Ugh. George felt like **he wanted to puke.**

"Get me out of here!" George shouted again.

"Somebody do something!" Mrs. Kelly called over to the museum workers.

Suddenly George felt someone yanking at his feet.

"George, can you hear me?" George

recognized that voice. It was Alex.

"Yes," George called back to him.

"Okay, try to wiggle yourself down while I pull," Alex said.

George wiggled and jiggled.

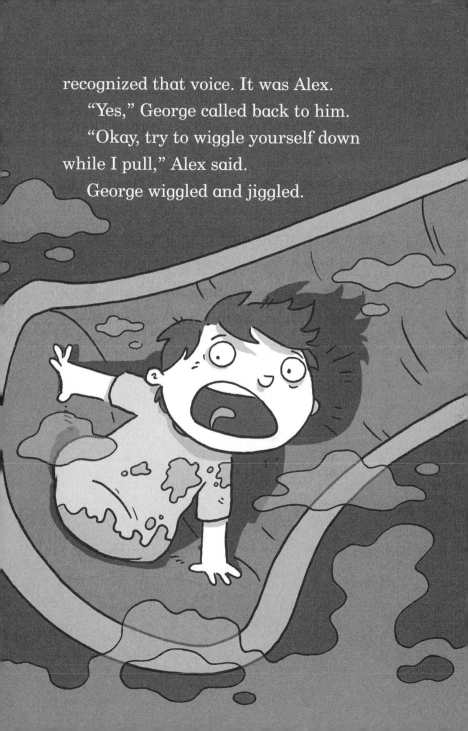

Alex pulled and yanked. But George didn't
go anywhere.

"I know how to get him out!" Julianna
shouted. She hurried to the top of the
nose and slid down the nostril. She flew
through the tiny nose hairs at top speed—
and stopped short when her sneakers hit
George's head.

"Ouch!"
George
shouted. "What
are you doing?"

"Trying to
get you out
of here,"
Julianna said.

"Well,
now we're
both stuck."
George
groaned.

Poof!
Just then,
another smell
filled the nostril.
It was all sweet
and flowery, like Mrs.
Kelly's stinky perfume.
Oh, great. Now George was
stuck inside a giant nostril with
Julianna's feet in his face and stinky
perfume all around him.

"It stinks in here!" George shouted
loudly.

"He's not kidding!" Julianna
added.

"Chris, come help me pull George's legs," Alex said. "You grab one. I'll grab the other."

"Whoa!" George shouted as he got yanked out of the nostril and landed with **a thud**—right on top of Chris and Alex.

"Yikes!" Julianna screamed as she slid out and landed on George.

George poked his head out from the people pile. "Thanks, guys," he told Chris, Julianna, and Alex. "I didn't think I was ever getting out of there."

Louie walked over to George. "So was that the weirdest thing that ever happened to you?"

George picked himself up. "Um, I don't know. Lots of weird stuff happens to me. **Like this one time at my old school** . . ." George was about to tell Louie about the time he got a purple jelly bean stuck up his nose. But he didn't get the chance.

"Yessss!" Louie shouted. He pumped his fist in the air. "You said it! I heard you! You said 'at my old school'!"

"He definitely said it," Max agreed.

"I heard you," Mike agreed. "*Everybody* heard you."

George looked at his friends. Chris, Julianna, and Alex were all nodding sadly.

Oh, man! George couldn't believe it. **He'd totally forgotten about the bet.** And now he was going to be Louie's servant for a whole day. Was that worse than being stuck in a giant nose?

George decided it was a toss-up.

Chapter 9

"Louie, you're up next," Julianna called from the pitcher's mound during gym class the next morning.

Louie walked over to home plate. "Come on, George," he called over to the bench.

"What?" George asked him. "I'm not up next."

"But you're my servant for the day," Louie explained. "So after I hit the ball, you're going to do all the running." He glared at George. "**And you'd better be fast.** I don't want our team to lose just because you run slowly."

George frowned. Louie was making him crazy. Already he'd made George hang up his coat in the coat closet, take all his really heavy books back to the library, and clean up his table after art class. Now he was making him run for him. **This was getting ridiculous.**

"Mr. Trainer will never go for this," George told Louie.

"Wanna bet?" Louie asked. He turned toward the first-base line where Mr. Trainer, the gym teacher, was standing. "Is it okay if George pinch-runs for me today?" he asked. "My foot hurts."

"Sure, Louie," Mr. Trainer said. "Just hit the ball."

Louie picked up the bat. Then he put it down again. "I call time-out."

"What's wrong?" Mr. Trainer asked.

"My shoelace is untied," Louie explained. He looked at George. **"Tie my lace, Servant for the Day."**

Grrr and double grrr.

Louie was really being

a jerk about this. Not that it was all that surprising. Louie was pretty much a jerk about everything.

George bent down and began to tie Louie's shoe.

"No, not that way," Louie said. "I always tie my shoes with the two bunny ears."

Triple grrr.

As soon as his shoelace was tied, Louie picked up his bat and got ready for Julianna's pitch.

THWACK

She wound up her arm
and let the ball fly toward
the plate.

"Miss, miss, miss," George wished
quietly under his breath. He didn't want
his team to lose, but he didn't want
Louie to get a good
hit, either.

SMACK! Louie
hit **a long drive**
into left field.

"Run!" Louie
ordered George.

George ran. He touched first base, made it to second, rounded third, and then . . . Julianna threw the ball toward home plate.

"Slide!" Louie shouted.

Rrrippp.

That was the sound of George's new jeans ripping as he slid toward home plate. Oh, man, **his mom was going to be so mad**.

"Safe!" Mr. Trainer shouted. "Good slide, George. You won the game for your team!"

"No, *I* won the game," Louie said. "He was pinch-running for me. It was my home run!"

"Either way, your team won."
Mr. Trainer looked at his watch. "Let's get inside, gang. Lunch is waiting."

"You'd better wash your hands before lunch," Louie told George. "I'm going to want you to cut my meat loaf for me. And you're a mess."

George rolled his eyes. This was the **longest day in history**. The only good thing was that, for once, the magic super burp had kept its distance.

Alex walked over to George. "I have a pair of sweatpants in my backpack," he told him. "They might fit you."

"Thanks." George smiled. He was glad Alex didn't mind having a best friend who burped.

"Oh, and I have another idea for getting rid of the super burp," Alex told him. **"Have you tried an onion milk shake?"**

George gave Alex a funny look. "That sounds disgusting."

"But onions help fight gas," Alex said. "And

milk coats your stomach, too. It might be worth a try."

George shrugged. Why not? Although George had a feeling that sooner or later, **the burp would be back**. And when it returned, it was sure to bring trouble. Ba-a-ad trouble!

About the Author

Nancy Krulik is the author of more than 150 books for children and young adults including three *New York Times* best sellers and the popular Katie Kazoo, Switcheroo books. She lives in New York City with her family, and many of George Brown's escapades are based on things her own kids have done. (No one delivers a good burp quite like Nancy's son, Ian!) Nancy's favorite thing to do is laugh, which comes in pretty handy when you're trying to write funny books!

About the Illustrator

Aaron Blecha was raised by a school of giant squid in Wisconsin and now lives with his family by the English seaside. He works as an artist designing toys, animating cartoons, and illustrating books, including the Zombiekins and The Rotten Adventures of Zachary Ruthless series. You can enjoy more of his weird creations at www.monstersquid.com.

George Brown,
CLASS CLOWN

Read all the books in the
GEORGE BROWN, CLASS CLOWN series!